D1577999

PRISONER OF STORM

The darkness held the faint white of falling snow, but was no less impenetrable for that. Yet some extrasensory warning prompted me to stare back into the gloom. Something moved there, something stalking me as a beast might stalk its prey! I shrieked hysterically and turned to run, and it was as though the desperation of my need guided me over the ice. I fled toward where Valhalla waited somewhere at the end of the road. Gradually, the slope became a cliff, and the sea on my right seemed louder, fiercer. Risking a look back, I screamed and ran still faster. He had almost overtaken me! Sobbing, I turned the corner and ran into the full force of the wind. And suddenly I was whirled up and around as though in some macabre dance that brought me closer and closer to the edge of the cliff. . . .

Other SIGNET Gothics by Caroline Farr

☐ **DARK CITADEL** (#Y7552—$1.25)

☐ **HEIRESS TO CORSAIR KEEP** (#W7980—$1.50)

☐ **THE HOUSE OF LANDSDOWN** (#W7700—$1.50)

☐ **SIGNET DOUBLE GOTHIC—A CASTLE IN SPAIN** and **SO NEAR AND YET . . .** (#E8057—$1.75)

☐ **SIGNET DOUBLE GOTHIC—HOUSE OF DARK ILLUSIONS** and **THE SECRET OF THE CHATEAU** (#E7662—$1.75)

☐ **SINISTER HOUSE** (#W7892—$1.50)

☐ **THE TOWERS OF FEAR** (#Y7001—$1.25)

THE NEW AMERICAN LIBRARY, INC.,
P.O. Box 999, Bergenfield, New Jersey 07621

Please send me the books I have checked above. I am enclosing $_____(check or money order—no currency or C.O.D.'s). Prices and numbers are subject to change without notice. Please include the list price plus the following amounts for postage and handling: 35¢ for Signets, Signet Classics, and Mentors; 50¢ for Plumes, Meridians, and Abrams.

Name_____

Address_____

City_____State_____Zip Code_____
Allow at least 4 weeks for delivery

House of Valhalla

by
Caroline Farr

A SIGNET BOOK
NEW AMERICAN LIBRARY
TIMES MIRROR

NAL BOOKS ARE ALSO AVAILABLE AT DISCOUNTS IN BULK
QUANTITY FOR INDUSTRIAL OR SALES-PROMOTIONAL USE.
FOR DETAILS, WRITE TO PREMIUM MARKETING DIVISION,
NEW AMERICAN LIBRARY, INC., 1301 AVENUE OF THE
AMERICAS, NEW YORK, NEW YORK 10019.

Copyright © 1978 by Horwitz Publications, a division of
Horwitz Group Books Pty. Ltd. (Hong Kong Branch), Hong
Kong B.C.C.

Reproduction in part or in whole in any language expressly forbidden in any part of the world without the written consent of
Horwitz Publications.

All rights reserved. For information address Horwitz Cammeray
Centre, 506 Miller Street, P.O. Box 306, Cammeray 2062,
Australia.

 SIGNET TRADEMARK REG. U.S. PAT. OFF. AND FOREIGN COUNTRIES
REGISTERED TRADEMARK—MARCA REGISTRADA
HECHO EN CHICAGO, U.S.A.

SIGNET, SIGNET CLASSICS, MENTOR, PLUME AND MERIDIAN BOOKS
are published by The New American Library, Inc.,
1301 Avenue of the Americas, New York, New York 10019

FIRST SIGNET PRINTING, JULY, 1978

1 2 3 4 5 6 7 8 9

PRINTED IN THE UNITED STATES OF AMERICA

★ 1 ★

The man sitting beside me on the plane said that it was snowing in Florida and the oranges were frozen on the trees. Our plane had been the last flight out that day because of the weather, and anytime I saw the ground as we crossed over the Midwest it was carpeted with snow. It was the kind of day you could believe anything about— even if someone told you an iceberg had been sighted in the Amazon. A day like that builds up tension in people, and when I left the airport and saw the antiquated bus that was to take me on the last stage of my journey to Fifeness, Maine, my tension increased.

I would have taken the next plane back to San Francisco if I could have, but that wasn't possible. I didn't have the return fare. Nor did I have a job or an apartment to return to. The firm of Sanders & Clayton, Publishers, for whom I'd worked as an editor for a year, had closed its doors. Two weeks later I had received a letter from Adrienne Courbet offering me a secretarial job under her boss, Johann Richter, in Fifeness. The letter had seemed a godsend.

The weather outside the bus windows was deteriorating. The thermometer kept right on dropping toward subzero as though the mercury were leaking from it. An icy North Atlantic wind kept pelting our bus with snow and sleet.

Conditions worsened with every slow mile we made toward Fifeness and the sea. Ice built on the outside of my window and the world beyond the bus vanished. I'd never seen weather like it.

It wasn't long before we came on a snowplow, and the bus was slowed to walking pace. I began to feel lonely and nervous as one after another relieved passenger dropped off where wayside lights gleamed and relatives waited with better transport to take them to such luxuries as hot drinks, hot food, hot baths, and warm beds.

The occupants of the bus had been reduced to three passengers and the tense driver. The other two, an elderly couple in the seat behind the driver, seemed to know him, for he had grumbled to them continuously until now. For the last twenty minutes or so, though, he hadn't spoken a word except to curse to himself each time the bus lurched and skidded and he had to drag it frantically back onto firm pavement. There was no longer the slightest glimmer of light to be seen outside the bus. It was as though we passed through a dark and empty land.

We started downhill suddenly, skidding on the frozen road surface, which did nothing for my ebbing morale. The reactions of the couple behind the driver didn't help any, for the man had his arm around the woman' shoulders comfortingly and their heads were bowed as though in prayer. The wind seemed to be strengthening terrifingly outside, and I began to hear a new sound above its keening—the roar of an angry sea in turmoil somewhere not far away.

I hoped the driver could see the road ahead! The windshield wipers were having difficulty clearing the glass.

To calm myself I took out Adrienne's letter to reread for the nth time. The weak bus lights made reading difficult, but I knew the contents word for word by now anyway.

I had met Adrienne Courbet in London two years earlier and we'd become friends at first sight. Adrienne, a nurse, had just completed her training and qualified at one of the great French hospitals. With the strain of hospital work and study over, she planned to go on vacation and travel throughout Europe, taking private nursing jobs to pay her way. We were the same age, twenty, and had quite a few other things in common, which we discovered over lunch in a little restaurant in Camden Town. I had majored in modern languages at the University of California and meant to spend my vacation practicing the spoken languages in preparation for further postgraduate studies. Instead, because of my chance meeting with Adrienne, I was to spend a year traveling in Europe with her working as an *au pair* girl. We made a good traveling combination. I, an American, was proficient in German, Greek, and Spanish. Adrienne was French, but spoke Italian fluently, and had some knowledge of German, though she needed help with English. Between us we spoke six languages, and by the year's end were both passably fluent in all of them.

Adrienne was a very good nurse, and I discovered to my surprise for the first time that I had some talent as a secretary. Physically, though, we were opposites. Adrienne is a brunette with sultry brown eyes. She is slender, small, and vivacious, with an elfin smile that men seem to find irresistible.

I'm taller, a gray-eyed blond, more serious than Adrienne, and certainly not as flirtatious, even though men, especially the European ones, seemed to like me.

We spent our year in Europe traveling and generally living it up. We worked only when we needed the money, and when we had it we rested in cities like Paris or Berlin or Vienna, or vacationed in the Mediterranean resorts along the Riviera or the Spanish Costa Brava.

But in the end, of course, we both had to return home. We parted with regret, for an ingredient of the good times had been our mutual compatibility. When I received Adrienne's letter a year later I knew at once that even if I had been secure in my job with Sanders & Clayton and the offer in the letter had been less generous, I would have had to go. We'd had too much fun in Europe together not to want to recreate that here.

I had never expected Adrienne to come to America. We were both too busy for letter-writing, so communication between us had lapsed and died long since. But now here she was in a place called Fifeness, Maine, where apparently she had arrived from Berlin months ago as nurse to elderly Johann Richter, a wealthy retired German industrialist. Johann, her letter informed me, was writing his memoirs and needed a secretary who must be completely trustworthy and capable of perfect translation from German to English.

Adrienne said she had thought of me at once, remembering the good times we'd had together, and had told the author about me. She said her employer was enthusiastic and wanted me to work for him. The job was mine, he told Adrienne. She said he was a most generous employer, though he expected people to work hard. She suggested I write to him in German.

That seemed a good idea, so I wrote back at once in German and within days received a reply offering me the job at more than twice my previous salary at Sanders & Clayton's, and enclosing a cashier's check for my traveling expenses.

But I was certainly having second thoughts as my bus skidded downhill toward the unseen sea that I was beginning to smell on the wind even inside the almost completely sealed bus. The bus gave a final drunken lurch and stopped abruptly. I put the letter back hastily into my handbag, with my heart thumping in fear. I had heard of people in the European Alps freezing to death when their bus broke down in a blizzard which could not have been any worse than this.

"Is something the matter?" I called anxiously.

"Far as we go!" he said grumpily, though I detected relief in his voice.

I stared in disbelief at the blackness beyond the iced window beside me. "*This* is Fifeness?" I asked incredulously. "I don't see any town lights!"

"Won't see none, miss!" the elderly male passenger said. "Blackout! Always happens in a storm like this. Figure the line's down someplace. Doubt they'll find out where before morning. But this is Fifeness, all right. Stopped right outside Jim Harkness' store, he did. Got oil lamps lit in there, Jim has."

Talking, he had been getting up stiffly, stretching arms and legs, and wincing as he did so. His wife was doing the same, but she had more compassion, for she asked, "Do you have someplace to go, miss? A body could perish on a night like this without shelter."

"Someone is meeting me, thank you," I reassured her, getting up to adjust my coat and scarf and fasten my gloves.

The driver was hauling out the last baggage from the compartment at the back of the bus. He dumped mine unceremoniously beside me.

"Come on, you people, all out!" he ordered impatiently. "Bad night for driving, in case you didn't notice. Still got to drive to the depot before I can go home!"

"We're on our way, Ed," the elderly man said. "Come on, Em!"

The cold air rushed in, damp against my face, as they opened the door. I picked up my bags as best I could. The driver was holding the door open and peering out. Beyond him I could see the front of a small store with dim lights burning inside.

"Don't see no car waiting for you," the driver said. "What did you say the name of the party was who's to pick you up? Know most of the folk hereabouts."

I hadn't said, but I told him now. "I'm going to the Richters' place. They said someone would meet me at the bus stop."

He shook his head. "You're going to Valhalla? Them foreigners are sure to be stormbound tonight in that big old house of theirs. Valhalla is more than five miles out of town along the cliff road, and that's a bad road at the best of times. Probably no way you can contact 'em tonight, either. When the lights are out in Fifeness, you can bet the storm's cut the phone lines to Valhalla!"

"Thank you, driver. Good night."

He had dumped my bags on the sidewalk near the store window and was hauling himself back into the bus. The door closed behind him, and if he replied, I didn't hear it. I looked around, leaning against the wind rushing up the street as the bus pulled away. It took effort just to stand, even though I was partly protected by the store's sturdy awning, which reached out over the sidewalk. The two other occupants of the bus, clinging to each other defensively, were disappearing into the very teeth of that biting wind which pelted me with flying particles of frozen snow. As I watched, they vanished like ghosts into a flurry of snow.

The store doors were closed against it, but oil lamps burned inside, and while I hesitated, fearing the store closed and empty, and myself stranded alone in this bleak place, I saw movement behind the counter at the back of the store. Someone was in there!

I picked up my bags as quickly as I could. The doors opened when I pushed them with my shoulder. Heavily laden, I staggered inside away from the bitter wind. It was warmer in there. Old-fashioned oil heaters glowed near the counter, and a young man was sipping steaming coffee at one of the small tables arranged in an annex. He looked up at me, startled, as I let the bags slip to the ground from my frozen fingers.

The storekeeper, white-haired and sturdy, was staring at me as curiously as the young man. Evidence, I decided, that in Fifeness strangers were rare.

"Thought only the Jennings couple would be fool enough to be on the bus tonight," he said grumpily, drawing heavy white eyebrows together as he surveyed me. "And them only because they must, since they live here."

"I'm beginning to wish I wasn't on it, Mr. Harkness!" I said. "I was to be met at the bus stop by someone from the Richter house, Valhalla. But I don't see any car. Have you seen anyone from Valhalla in town this evening?"

He shook his head and glanced at the young man in the annex. "You see anyone?"

"I noticed Paul Richter at the gas station, but that was early this afternoon before the wind came up." The young man stood up and was coming over politely.

"Maybe he's still in town?" I said hopefully.

"Came into the store and bought cigarettes," the storekeeper said. "Soon as he'd lit one, he drove into the cliff road and went off home."

"Can I phone to let them know I'm here?"

"Line's cut," the storekeeper said laconically, verifying the bus driver's unhelpful prophecy. "Do no good if it wasn't. Nobody in their right mind going to travel that road tonight. The best thing for you to do is go see the widow Clout. She runs a boardinghouse, the only one in town. Price is reasonable, food good, and her house clean as a new pin. This could blow itself out tomorrow, or it could blow for a week. You never can tell. No doubt, if the Richters are expecting you, they'll send someone to pick you up soon as they can. They're human, after all, though there are some people in Fifeness doubt it."

I looked down at my bags, wondering how I was to carry them, and how far away the widow Clout's place might be.

"Is it far?"

"Block away." He looked at the young man. "This here is Rick Byron. No doubt he'll be glad to show you where the widow's place is, since he's one of her boarders. And being an artist, he has more time on his hands to do such things than other honest, hard-working people around here."

The young man grinned good-humoredly, ignoring the insult.

"Glad to," he said cheerfully, picking up my bags. "I'll bet you're tired and frozen. I'd offer to buy you a coffee, but you'll get a hot meal at the widow's place, and we've just time to get there before dinner. She likes us to be punctual."

I followed him out into the cold, and winced. If anything, the wind was stronger than before, the sleet and ice driving before it thicker. He chuckled, studying my expression. Except for the store, the shops were closed and dark.

"Cheer up! We'll be there in five minutes even in this!" He had to shout to make himself heard. "There's a log fire waiting for us at the widow's, and a hot meal. In winter there's always hot coffee. She makes the best brew in these parts."

"That man was rude to you!"

"It's just Jim's way," he said in the storekeeper's defense. "They're like that here in the East. Unless you were born here, or until they accept you as though you were . . ." He broke off. A gust of wind almost knocked me down. I cried out in fright as the sleet it carried lashed at my face. "Hold onto my arm!" he yelled. "The corner of our street is just ahead, and we'll be protected there."

I grabbed his arm in a death grip, with my heart thumping in my breast. Momentarily as the wind struck me I had the feeling I was being lifted and blown away. There was reassurance in gripping his arm. My scarf had gone, blown away, I realized as I felt the chill of its loss. A rowdy clanking sound started somewhere downhill from us, and something metallic hurtled past unseen in the darkness on the other side of the street. Its clangor stopped abruptly, as though it had been blown against one of the buildings over there.

"What was that?" I cried in fright.

"God knows! In here! Quick! This is getting serious!" Clinging desperately to his arm, I was being towed and pushed to the side. Miraculously we had our backs against the tall stone wall of a house. The wind howled more furiously than before past our corner. More debris was being hurled violently and even more noisily along the street we had just left. But here the wind had less force, and the bulk of the house protected us completely from the sleet.

"We'll shelter here for a while!" he shouted above the turmoil. "That was someone's roof going past. The poor devils will have some cleaning up to do when this is over! When one sheet of iron is torn from a roof in wind like this, it all goes!" He was putting down my bags, and I had to release his arm. He stretched his arms gratefully. "What did you pack in these, lead weights?"

"Just all my worldly possessions," I said.

He bent closer to see my face. "You're going to live permanently with the Richters? Are you a relative? You don't have any accent."

"Of course I don't!" I said indignantly. "I'm as American as you are! I'm going to work there as Mr. Richter's secretary. He's writing a book."

"Really?!" he said, grinning. He held out his hand to me. "Meet a fellow worker! He commissioned me to paint his portrait for the book's cover." He broke off abruptly. "What fool's out driving tonight?"

I had seen the lights coming erratically toward

the store. "It has to be someone looking for me. I told you they were to meet me here!"

"It would have to be Paul, then," he said. "Only Paul Richter would be so crazy as to drive that road on a night like this! I'm not sure you should go with him! You'd be safer at Mrs. Clout's place!"

"He won't find me here!" I panicked. "We'll have to go back."

"He's stopping at the store," he said, peering through the murk. "Harkness will tell him you're on your way to the widow's place. He can't miss seeing you, and it will be easier for him to pick you up here."

Staring with him, I watched a dark figure dash into the store and return as though he had not a moment to waste. The lights began to move again, approaching us.

"It's Paul," the young man beside me said, and I detected disappointment in his tone. "Will I see you again? Who shall I ask for?"

"I thought you said you were painting Mr. Richter's portrait?" I asked suspiciously, remembering things I'd learned about young men like this in Europe.

He laughed and bent his head to see me better. "Sorry! I haven't got used to the idea yet! I haven't even started to plan the portrait. You see, he only asked me yesterday!"

I smiled. I was not sure why, but the prospect of seeing him again was pleasing. But the vehicle, a jeep, was turning the corner. The lights shone full upon us, and Rick Byron waved it down quickly. "Tell him I'm Lorna Mitchell," I said.

He started to say something, but like an echo the dark figure beneath the jeep's canvas shouted: "Lorna Mitchell?"

"Yes?"

"I'm Paul Richter," the voice said curtly. "Get in! You can throw her things in the back, Byron. And make it fast, the weather is too bad to waste time."

There was resentment in the accented voice as he spoke to Rick. The accent was German, well-educated German. But his manners had been neglected, I decided, as Rick Byron put my gear in the back and politely helped me into the seat beside the driver.

"Mr. Byron has been most helpful," I said indignantly. "Thank you, Mr. Byron."

"You're welcome," Rick Byron said, obviously annoyed. He nodded curtly to Paul Richter and turned, hunched, into the storm.

"Don't make the mistake of fraternizing with such people, Fräulein," Paul Richter said arrogantly in German, beginning to turn the jeep. "Their ways are not our ways. Our household has no friends in Fifeness. The people here are ignorant, narrow-minded peasants. The man who just left you is another hippie, as you Americans call your city dropouts. He claims to be an artist, but I have seen some of his daubs and they are without talent. It would bring you no credit with my father if he knew you associated with such people."

"Then why has your father commissioned Herr

Byron to paint his portrait for the cover of the book he's writing?" I asked him.

"*What*?" The jeep lurched, turning, and his angry voice frightened me.

"He said your father commissioned the portrait yesterday." I hoped what I said wouldn't lose the artist his commission, but I had gone too far to stop.

"He lied!" he shouted angrily.

"I don't think he did. Why should he? For what reason, Herr Richter?"

"To impress a pretty girl, no doubt!" he said in a furious voice. He glared at me, holding the jeep stationary, barely protected by the corner of the house. "I know nothing of any such commission!"

I shrugged. "He seemed truthful to me. Could your father have commissioned him and not yet told you? It happened only yesterday, he said."

His anger came under control abruptly, but it was still there, directed against me now. "My father has become a foolish old man, Fräulein," he said. "One who must be protected against himself now that he is in his dotage. Since his senility seems worsening, I suppose it is possible that he hired the man without consulting me or asking my approval—in the same way that he hired you!"

He gave me no chance to retort, even if I hadn't been shocked into silence by the venom in his voice as he said it. He thrust the jeep violently into gear so that we leaped out from our sheltered corner and almost overturned as we were struck by the unbroken force of the gale. Even though I hung on desperately, it nearly plucked me from my seat, until I saw that he was belted into his seat, and groping frantically, I managed to find and lock my own seat belt.

With the wind from behind pushing us, the jeep bounded up the hill like a frightened jack-rabbit. Outside the store we turned abruptly right, with the wind blowing full upon me where I sat behind the flapping canvas side curtain. The cold and the wind took my breath away, so that I could not cry out in protest or answer the bullying questions he was shouting at me as the dim lamp-lights of the store vanished quickly behind us. Terrified, cold, whipped by the full violence of the gale now, I would have given anything I possessed to be safe in the warmth and comfort of the widow Clout's boardinghouse with Rick Byron.

Chains around the jeep's tires clanked as we drove, the sound barely noticed in the growing fury around us. We must be close to the sea; its angry roaring seemed almost beneath us. The jeep's lights stabbed weakly at the white gloom ahead. How he could keep the car on the road I had no idea, for already the freezing snow covered it. Then I noticed the rapidly vanishing twin depressions the jeep's tires had made as he drove to Fifeness to pick me up. When they disappeared . . .

His angry voice jolted me out of my terror.

"What makes you think *you* are capable of preparing the manuscript of my father's memoirs?" his voice roared above the gale. "You were little better than a typist when the Courbet girl knew you in Europe."

"I've been doing the same kind of work with a California publisher!" I screamed back at him, gripping my seat with both hands. "Editing, translating, and preparing manuscripts, some in German. I was a secretary in Europe—not a typist. I speak and write German!"

"Your spoken German leaves a lot to be desired," he roared. "The old man's English is about as good as your German. You'll find whole passages of his memoirs still in German, which he'll expect you to translate into faultless English. What makes you think you are capable of doing that?"

I gasped. Ahead on my side of the road, if it could be called that, a yawning abyss had appeared. To make it worse, high ground on the left of the road loomed suddenly higher, becoming a cliff face rising from the very edge of the road. "Look where you're going!" I shrieked. "This is no place to argue my qualifications!"

"Where did you meet Adrienne Courbet?"

"London!" I cried in terror, for ahead the abyss and the cliff were converging; between them, a flat ledge carpeted in white that looked little wider than the jeep led away into infinity. "Stop! Please, I want to get out! I'm frightened! The road's too narrow!"

"So you became *au pair* girls? How long were you together?"

"A year! Please! Let me walk! I'm . . . scared!"

"You know Stuttgart? You worked there? Where my father had his factories?"

"*Yes.* But I've never heard of your father's factories." I began to tug at the canvas. A stud pulled free, and snow and sleet falling from the canvas roof were driven into the jeep, filling my lap with freezing white.

"He told you what the memoirs are about, didn't he, when he wrote to you?"

"No! No, he didn't."

"But he told you why he wants to write them? He told you that?"

"No! Nothing. Please let me . . ."

"If you open that door and get out," he said grimly, "you'll be dead, Fräulein Mitchell. *Don't!*"

Ahead, the snow-covered ledge we traveled upon seemed to end in blackness, the blackness of night and the abyss falling away to the angry sea below. Through the opening in the canvas as I peered down I saw the edge, no more than inches from the slowly turning tires on my side. I had meant to get out. I changed my mind hurriedly. And as I stared petrified at the menace ahead and below, out of the black nothing white foam spurted high, spattering the road and the cliff wall with droplets of seawater that stuck and froze on impact, adding to the peril.

I stared at my driver in horror. He must be mad, utterly mad. As Rick Byron had said, no sane person would have driven me to this awful place tonight.

"Stop!" I screamed, with hysteria close. "The road ends ahead! Can't you see? We'll be killed!"

"Come, now!" he demanded fiercely. "What did

my father tell you about this book you are to type and translate?"

"Nothing! He told me *nothing*! Please stop! I'm scared, I want to get out!" I cried, terrified.

"You lie!" he accused me grimly. "You have intelligence, your friend Adrienne says. Would any intelligent girl travel across a continent to a job she knew nothing about? Would she come here not knowing what her employer expected of her? I am not a fool, Fräulein. I want the truth from you. Now!"

I could not answer. I was too terrified to retort. The dark edge of the road ahead was coming closer. I was sure we were about to fall. I dared not jump; the edge was too close to my side of the jeep. The maelstrom of gale-tormented sea waited far below. And suddenly the jeep began to turn, rounding a previously unseen curve in the cliff face. The road ahead seemed wider, straighter, safer. The corner behind that had so terrified me now partly shielded us from the wind and the sleet.

I let my breath gush out in relief. "I've no idea why your father is writing his memoirs. Or what he is writing about. But you should know that if I am his secretary and he does not want others to know this, then I will never tell you or anyone else."

"You think of yourself as stubborn, eh?"

"Mr. Richter, this is what being a good secretary is all about. Her employer must be able to trust her. Surely you know that?"

"I have known other kinds," he said. He added menacingly, "And as for you . . ."

As he spoke, the motor coughed and died. In the silence the sounds of the storm seemed louder and more frightening suddenly.

"What's the matter?" I cried in fright.

"Stalled!" he said. He jabbed at the starter. The starter whined futilely again and again while his anger grew, and my fear with it. Its whirring weakened, faded, died as it ground to a standstill. The jeep's lights died with it, leaving us in the utter dark.

He cursed in German. "The battery's dead!" he said disgustedly. "In this country one should never trust servants, but must do everything oneself! I ordered a new battery in town today. The chauffeur was to bring it home and install it. He did not!"

"What . . . will we do now?" I cried in fright as the wind whipping the curtain on my side showed me the cliff edge closer than I had thought. "Can we push it in gear to start it?"

He shook his head and opened the door on his side, letting in cold air. "Too dangerous! This is the safest and most sheltered part of the road, but if we pushed it in this storm the jeep or one of us could be blown over the edge. Connell, the chauffeur, has the battery. He lives just off the road not far from here. I'll get it!"

He had closed the door before the implication of what he meant registered in my mind, multiplying my terror. "*Wait!*" I yelled. "I'm not staying here alone!"

"You're safe there," his voice called back, already faint. "You might not be safe where I'm going. I'll return in a few minutes. But don't leave the jeep. That's an order!"

He was gone, and in the darkness I had no way of knowing which way. Ahead, I presumed, but was not sure. I yelled again, frantically, but he did not answer.

★ 2 ★

I huddled alone in the jeep that seemed to have a life of its own, for it moved when heavier gusts of wind pried into our sheltered stretch of road. In the darkness I searched my luggage in the back and managed to find several sweaters and my down jacket. Some I put on, others I wrapped around me in a cocoon that seemed to open every now and then when I moved, to let in the bitter, freezing cold.

My terror at being abandoned in this awful place had become an apathy of dazed acceptance when I discovered that I could neither find nor recall the man who had left me here alone. At first I ached with the cold; my ears and fingers and toes tingled and became numb. I huddled in my cocoon of clothing, every sense taut, searching for the return of Paul Richter and the battery. How long I remained like this I had no idea, but I was sure it was much longer than the "few minutes" Paul Richter had assured me he would go away. Much, much more!

Only, strangely now, these things were beginning to seem unimportant. I began to feel warmer and less afraid, even though I was vaguely aware that the storm was worsening. Of such a degree of cold I had no recent experience, but vague memories were beginning to prod my numbed mind warningly. This new warmth, this languor, could be the anesthesia of freezing. It had happened this way to people snowbound in the Alps the year I was in Europe. A survivor interviewed on television had spoken of the delicious feeling of warmth that enveloped him just before rescuers found him unconscious.

The rest of his party hadn't been so lucky. They were past revival. And so would I be, I realized vaguely, if I didn't do something about it. My drowsiness, like theirs, could be the prelude to the sleep of death.

A fiercer gust of wind rocked the jeep violently, helping revive me, starting me thinking again. I realized that I was clinging to the seat of the rocking vehicle. It was too close to the edge, and it was being pelted with sleet. Ice plated the windshield and was building rapidly upon both the jeep itself and the cliff road. I could not wait for Paul Richter, as he had ordered, for to stay here was to die; I was becoming sure of that. My terror came back, intensified by the fear of death.

A flurry of snow carried on the wind enveloped me as I struggled with numb fingers to open the door on the driver's side, for the edge was too close to use my own door. I met unexpected resistance as I pushed and struggled. Ice, unnoticed, had built across the doorjamb, sealing it fast. When it gave unexpectedly with the crackling sound of breaking glass, I fell clumsily from the jeep onto the frozen snow and sleet covering the road. I struggled to my feet with difficulty.

I had lost part of my cocoon of clothing. I groped for what I could find with gloved fingers stiffened within their protective covering, and threw several sweaters into the back of the jeep. The darkness held the faint white of falling snow but was no less impenetrable for that. I hesitated, clinging to the jeep, while the wind swept past and sleet stung my exposed face. Despite my desperate situation, I was reluctant to leave. The jeep was familiar. Along this awful road ahead lay the unknown. I was not sure whether Paul Richter had gone back or forward. All I could be sure of was that Valhalla, the Richter house, should be somewhere in the direction the jeep pointed its snub nose.

And while I vacillated, some extrasensory warning prompted me to stare back into the gloom toward the curve we had come around. Something moved there, vaguely seen. Something creeping toward the jeep from behind, something stalking me as a beast might stalk its prey!

My heart started a sick thumping as I called quaveringly, "Who's there? Is that you, Mr. Richter?"

The stealthy movement stopped at once, immobilized by my voice, but only waiting for my attention to be diverted from it, as a hunter might wait. I strained my eyes to see it better, but could not see it at all now that it was still.

"*Mr. Richter!*" I screamed. "Is that you?"

There was no movement back there in the gloom. Nothing. Whatever I had seen, I decided, had not been Paul Richter. Back there had been only the cliff above us and the abyss and the sea below. There was no side road there leading to anyone's house. Not to the house of the Richter's chauffeur or anyone else. If there was such a house, such a side road, it could only be somewhere ahead.

And as I stared back, trembling, the furtive movement started again, barely noticeable—but it was moving as stealthily as before toward me.

And suddenly the day's events overwhelmed me—the frightening bus ride, the flying debris of destroyed houses in the village, my cruel abandonment, and now a predator creeping upon me out of the gale-tortured night.

I shrieked hysterically and turned to run, but my leather shoes slipped from beneath me on the icy surface and I fell heavily. I scrambled up and stared back in terror, seeing my pursuer closer now, and human. A man's voice shouted angrily, the words muffled, as vague and unrecognizable as the man himself. Turning in terror to run, I remembered my fall. I forced myself to be cautious, to step more warily. He was coming fast, making the same mistake in his eagerness that I in my abject terror had made, and inevitably it had the same result. I heard his startled cry as he too slipped and fell. And by then, becoming more surefooted as I went, I was leaving him behind.

It was as though the desperation of my need guided me over the ice. I could no longer hear him behind me, and the road here was widening, the cliff becoming a steep slope above me. I came to the vague trace of a track leading away into a small valley. This, I decided, must be the side-track Paul Richter had said led to the chauffeur's house. But if there was a house in there, it burned no lights tonight. Nor could I see or hear Paul Richter returning as he had promised. Surely he would have obtained a flashlight from the chauffeur? But in there seemed only darkness, and the sound of wind boring bleakly through a narrow place.

Perhaps, seeing no lights, Paul Richter had gone on to Valhalla? The Richter house could not be far away. Five miles from the village, the bus driver said. Valhalla must be within easy walking distance from where I stood vacillating like a frightened child. I looked back and repressed a scream. My pursuer was still coming after me relentlessly. He was quite close, but he seemed uncertain, for he was slowing, moving closer to the high ground above where I stood.

I decided he must know about the side road, and was trying to make up his mind which way I would go. With my terror coming back I fled toward where Valhálla waited somewhere at the end of the road. I went stealthily at first, as fast as I could without falling, but making no sound other than my heavy breathing, which was partly out of fear and partly out of exhaustion.

I ran on, slipping, panting, but with panic driving me. The road was easier, but I was leaving the break in the cliff and the side road behind. The slope had become a cliff again, looming high above the road, and the sea on my right now seemed louder, fiercer again as I ran. Ahead I began to see what looked like the end of the road, for there was only darkness and the turbulent sound of the sea beyond.

I had seen nothing of my pursuer since leaving the sidetrack. I slowed instinctively, feeling safer, wishfully thinking that perhaps he had taken the other track. Looking back, I shrieked in terror and started running again. He had almost overtaken me! He hadn't been fooled by the side road and had correctly guessed what I would do. I could hear him close behind me as I ran for the turn in the road ahead. I ran desperately, forgetting all my former caution. Sobbing, I turned the corner and ran into the full force of the wind, feeling its furious blast on my body. I was whirled around as though in some macabre dance. Unable to stand, I staggered and fell.

I screamed. It was as though I was being lifted bodily. My gloved fingers and booted feet scrabbled at the icy surface but could find no grip. Sliding across ice, I was thrown hard against a rock face that drove the breath from my body. Somewhere, like an echo to my scream, I was aware of a male voice.

I began to realize that I had been thrown across the road against the cliff wall. I was lying there dazed, sheltered for the moment, but in my dark clothing against the frozen snow I must be seen if my pursuer came this way. And he could not be far off. I heard his voice again, like the mewing of a gull barely heard above the awful wind that howled in frustration as it tried vainly to tear me from the cliff and throw me into the sea. Instinctively, I clung to a crevice in the rock, but my gloved fingers were weakening, cramping, threatening to let go.

I dragged myself upright painfully, and stood there gripping the rock while the wind tugged and tormented me. Of my pursuer I could see and hear nothing now. Searching out what holds I could find with frozen fingers, I began to edge an inch at a time along the cliff face. Road and cliff were curving sharply ahead, so that as I crept along the side of the road the howling wind seemed to attack me from different angles, each more difficult to resist than the last. I forgot the vague figure of a man from whom I had fled, in the greater danger of this terrible wind threatening imminently to destroy me.

Ahead I began to see more clearly the next corner in this awful road, a corner that I approached in terror now. I glanced back fearfully, but could see no pursuing figure, hear no sound of his coming. I wondered if, hearing my terrified scream as the wind almost blew me into the sea, he had turned back. Or perhaps he had not been as lucky as I, and had himself been blown into the sea.

I reached the corner, and clung there trying to gather courage to fight a wind coming from some new and perhaps even more violent direction. But was it possible for wind to reach a greater violence than what I was already experiencing? For, as though made desperate by the possibility of my escape, it was attacking me again with increasing fury. If I did not turn the corner now, it might drive me into the sea that waited directly ahead, that here was as noisy and turbulent as the wind. My fingers gripping the rock were weakening; so were my legs. I told myself it must be now or never.

Sobbing, I dragged myself the last few feet, squirming around a sharp corner of rock, into a curve that ahead became a straight stretch of road. Miraculously, it seemed, the power of the wind here was less, the turmoil and the noise abating. The road stretched away ahead—still a cliff road with the sea below, but calmer, safer.

I looked up and saw the lights.

They rose distantly ahead on ground where the bluff seemed to become lesser hills leading away from the sea. I could see the vague shape of the big house behind the lights that rose in tiers three stories high. As lights they were poor enough, with none of the clear brightness of normal electricity. The blackout the bus driver had warned me about must still be on here. But these had to be the lights of Valhalla, home of the Richter family, the place where my friend Adrienne Courbet lived.

I was not yet free of the awful wind, except in a matter of degree. But it had lost its power to browbeat and terrify me. I felt I had survived the worst that it could do, so my fear of it was gone. My goal was in sight ahead: Valhalla. Adrienne waited there, and safety. I staggered toward those lights on shaking legs. Womanlike, I suppose, in my reaction, I began to cry.

Tall, strong gates of iron took shape as I approached, gates with spikes upon their bars, like the gates of some fortress or prison. But after the darkness of that awful road, the reassuring lights of Valhalla were like a wonderland. The gates stood open, as though waiting for me, and there was a light in the window of the neat white-painted cottage beside them. Sparks glittered, rising from the cottage chimney. But I did not disturb the gatekeeper within, whom in my chilled state I enviously pictured sitting over a bright fire smoking his evening pipe.

A drive led between leafless winter trees to the great house, and if the gatekeeper's cottage was cozy, there must be warmth and light there too. The grounds were white; frozen snow and ice clung to the stronger branches of the trees lining the drive, despite the wind. The drive was treacherous beneath my feet, and ice crusted the steps and framed the windows of the mansion.

I had not realized how completely exhausted I was until I began to climb the wide steps of Valhalla that led up to a massive door with a welcoming light above it. Sobbing in relief, I pressed the button and listened to musical chimes start somewhere within, the sound muted by the massive door. At least this was a modern household, I decided. They had a chiming doorbell and a private source of electricity. For though the light above the door was weak, it was an electric bulb glowing up there. The electricity had to be generated by an auxiliary power plant. I could hear it thumping steady as a heartbeat somewhere behind the great house.

I was not sure what I had expected to find here after what I had experienced on the way. Oil lamps, perhaps, like they had in Fifeness village? A crumbling ruin for a house? A sinister butler like the type they used in horror movies to welcome unsuspecting strangers like me? The door began to open, and I stepped back involuntarily in fright at the thought.

Instead, a blond and blue-eyed girl in a housemaid's uniform opened the door and looked out at me, and behind her I saw a dark-haired young woman come out of one of the passage doors and run to meet me. After that, I saw only the second girl. *Adrienne!*

We were hugging each other, the maid forgotten in our reunion. I cried, and Adrienne's laughter sounded close to tears too. It was the maid who brought us back to our senses.

"What has happened to the Fräulein's luggage, Fräulein Courbet?" she asked in German, staring down the steps nervously at the empty drive. "I can't see Herr Richter or the jeep. Has he driven it to the back door?"

Adrienne released me abruptly to stare at me in consternation. "You're half-frozen, Lorna, and you look terrible. What has happened? Where is Paul? How did you get here?"

Words gushed from me as I began to tell her, but I did not get very far.

A stern male voice called in German from one

of the doors along the passage, "What are you foolish women doing out there letting in the cold? Bring the girl in here, Nurse Courbet—if it is your friend Fräulein Mitchell?"

Adrienne glanced at me and laughed. "Coming, Herr Richter!" she called. She caught my arm and whispered, "That is the voice of your future boss, Lorna! And you do what he says—so come on! He doesn't like to be kept waiting."

"And shut that door!" the stern voice ordered.

The maid closed it hurriedly as Adrienne led me toward the sound of my new employer's voice. "We've got to get you out of those frozen clothes and warmed, Lorna!" she muttered in alarm, feeling the sleeve of my coat. "You'll catch pneumonia! How did you get yourself in this state?"

"Walking," I said. "Or rather running! I was trying to run away from something that frightened me. . . ."

"You always had too much imagination," she said. "You said the jeep broke down and Paul went for help? Why didn't you stay in the jeep?" She was steering me into a huge room. I felt its warmth as we entered. A log fire burned in an open hearth, and in a deep leather chair near it a huge old man with a shock of white hair was sipping a hot drink, his gnarled hands clasping the hot glass tightly.

"The jeep broke down?" the old man said, turning his head just far enough for him to be able to study me from beneath beetling white brows. "Impossible!"

"This is my friend Lorna Mitchell, Herr

Richter," Adrienne said, and explained for me: "She said the jeep stalled on the cliff road. When Paul tried to start it, he discovered the battery was dead. He told Lorna to stay in the jeep while he walked to the Connell house for a battery, but she became frightened alone and . . . well, she walked here. . . ."

The shaggy white head turned to see me better, and he was staring at me, seeing me for the first time. "Tonight? She *walked*?"

Adrienne nodded. "Yes, Herr Richter."
blue eyes, I saw, could still be alert and curious.

"Why?" The question was for me. The faded

"Your son said he would only be a few minutes, Herr Richter. It seemed as though I sat in the jeep alone for a long time. When I found I was falling asleep, I thought . . . Anyway, I got out to start walking. Then I saw someone coming from . . . the direction of the village. I called out asking if it was Herr Richter. I called out twice, but there was no answer, so I ran away. . . . I came here."

"*Where* did this happen?"

"I don't know how to tell you where. We had rounded a bend, and it was sheltered where the jeep stalled. Walking, I passed the turnoff to the chauffeur's house, I think. Then I came to another corner and was almost blown into the sea!"

"You never saw Paul, my son?"

"No."

"People imagine things when they are about to perish in the snow," he said grimly. "Nobody from the village would follow the jeep tonight. No doubt Paul is looking for you back there on the cliff road at this moment."

"When you called us, I was about to tell Lorna that she took a foolish risk in leaving the jeep, Herr Richter," Adrienne said placatively. "She could have been killed! In a storm like tonight's, that part of the road isn't called the Devil's Bend for nothing. Others have died there, I've been told, blown from the cliff in their vehicles. To leave a vehicle and walk was suicidal!"

"Nevertheless, Nurse Courbet," the old man said harshly, "she is here, and she is alive. If she had stayed in the jeep, Paul would be finding her now, I think. Dead."

I shuddered at the grim certainty in his voice, but Adrienne was pointing at the window where light danced suddenly on the frosted glass. "The jeep is coming, Herr Richter! It's Paul, driving fast!" Adrienne said in a relieved voice. "He's safe too."

"I never doubted that," the old man said. He looked at the hovering maid. "A glass of this for Fräulein Mitchell, Elsa. It will drive the chill from her bones."

"Ja, Herr Richter!" The girl smiled at me and hurried to her wheeled tray, where an urn steamed.

"You see?" Adrienne said, still staring at the oncoming lights reflected dimly on the windows. "Paul has done exactly what he said, Lorna. He will be sick with worry. He will think you have had an accident at the Devil's Bend!"

"Fräulein."

The maid had brought me the hot drink. The glass was so hot I could barely hold it, and the tang of the alcohol in it caught my breath. Sipping, I studied Johann Richter unobtrusively. His body I saw now was but the shadow of what must once have been a huge, strong man. Whatever illness he had contracted had reduced him to skeletal proportions. In his lined face only the eyes seemed living and alert. He looked more like an aged corpse that refused to accept death than a living, breathing man. I found him frightening. Though Adrienne, his nurse, seemed quite undisturbed and at home in his presence.

The lights of the jeep were switched off. I heard the chimes again, louder and more musical. Paul Richter was coming. I braced myself nervously for the approaching confrontation. I heard his footsteps in the passage then, and he came in quickly. He did not see me at first, nor could I see his face where I sat, with his father and Adrienne between us.

"There has been an accident, Father!" he blurted out angrily. "The jeep broke down just before the Devil's Bend, and the stupid girl wandered away while I was walking to Connell's house for a new battery. I heard her scream as I was returning with the battery. I put the battery down and ran, but she's gone! I searched and shouted, but I can't find her. She must have been . . ."

He broke off abruptly as he saw me. His face changed, became paler I thought. "I began to feel sleepy," I said apologetically. "I became frightened. I thought I'd freeze, and you were a long time away, Herr Richter."

He shook his head, recovering from the shock of seeing me. "*You're safe?*" he said, his voice still angry. "I heard you scream, and thought you fell! Of course I was a long time away! You know the kind of night it was."

"An accident, you say, Paul?" A younger man had entered the room behind Paul and was studying him suspiciously. A younger edition of Paul, but with dark hair and eyes.

Paul glanced at him angrily. "Yes, an accident, I said, Herman! If you can call her stupidity in leaving the jeep against my direct orders an accident? But fortunately one without ill effects—as you see. For which I'm grateful, since I would have felt guilty if she was in the sea."

"As you should," Herman said, turning away toward the maid. "You should have left her in the village till morning. She would have been safe there. Elsa, I'll have one of those, thank you. Hot and strong. It's been a trying night."

"I'm glad you survived your mistake, Miss Mitchell." Paul Richter gave me a thin smile. "You gave me some bad moments." He turned to the maid. "I'll have the same, Elsa, and my need is greater than Herman's, after what Miss Mitchell did to me."

Herman stepped back to allow the maid to serve his brother first. He smiled at Adrienne, and I noticed how Adrienne positively purred when he looked at her. "Father," he said, "your new secretary looks half frozen. Adrienne should take her upstairs for a hot bath and change of clothing after her frightening experience."

The old man nodded and studied me briefly. "Look after your friend, Nurse Courbet," he ordered. "Where are your clothes, Fräulein?"

I looked at Paul coming back to the fire with his hot drink, and he said grimly, "I left her luggage in the jeep, Father, believing she had no further use for it."

"Get it!" the old man snapped. "Elsa, have someone take the Fräulein's luggage to her room."

Paul shrugged silently, drained his glass, and stalked obediently out into the passage. The old man was getting up with difficulty, and Adrienne was urging me out of my chair. It was evident that whether he was sick or not, Johann Richter gave the orders in Valhalla.

"It's going to be wonderful having you here, Lorna," Adrienne said as we left the room together. "There's so much I want to tell you! It will be like old times, you'll see!"

"I hope so," I said doubtfully. I couldn't really consider my introduction to Valhalla and the Richters welcoming.

"You'll like Paul and Herman," she said. "And Herr Richter senior is okay when you get used to his ways. As his nurse, I know!"

I lowered my voice as we began to climb the stairs. "What happened to the father, Adrienne? He looks terrible. Yet his mind seems clear enough."

"It is," she said, and lowered her voice to a

whisper. "But he has an inoperable brain tumor, and the condition is terminal, the doctors say. At most he has only six months, yet he's determined to see his memoirs in print."

"Maybe that's what is keeping the poor man alive," I suggested, shocked.

"Maybe," she agreed. "He's been working on his memoirs for five years, Herman says. Herman is against the project, though not as much as Paul. But we're going to have plenty of time to talk about things like that, Lorna. I went to work for Johann in Stuttgart just after you left Europe, when I heard the family wanted a nurse to go to America with them. I missed you and I thought if I came to America we could get together again when Johann died. I kept meaning to write to you when we did get here. But I got involved here, and just didn't get around to writing until Johann said you could have the secretarial job."

I thought I knew what the "involvement" was, knowing Adrienne. "You like Herman, don't you?"

"Does that show?" she asked, surprised.

I almost laughed. "To someone who knows you as well as I do—yes."

"So okay," Adrienne confided in a low voice as we reached the landing and she led me toward my room. "I'm in love with Herman, and I intend to marry him. Before the old man dies, if I can, because I'd sooner have his approval. Johann is a family man, and he'd favor his married son if one married before he died."

I giggled involuntarily. "You still have the practicability of a Frenchwoman, I see, Adrienne!"

"But of course," she said, surprised that I might have doubted it. She glanced around conspiratorially. "Lorna, why don't you grab Paul? As the eldest son, he must become even more wealthy than Herman when the old man dies." Fitting a key into a door, she added thoughtfully, "Paul would be susceptible to a girl like you. You're a blond, and attractive. Herman says Paul went for the Aryan breeding theory the Nazis favored. And to my knowledge Paul hasn't looked at a woman since we left Germany."

"*You* haven't changed, Adrienne!" I told her, amused. "Even if I could forgive him for deserting me on that awful road tonight and scaring me the way he did, I wouldn't marry him if he was the *last* man on earth. He's just everything I wouldn't want! He's bad-tempered and arrogant, he's domineering and . . . and untrustworthy! And I don't care if his father is a millionaire. And besides, he's too old, he must be fifty!"

"Fifty-six," Adrienne said. "And Johann isn't just a millionaire, he is that many times over. So why don't you just keep an open mind about Paul, eh, Lorna? Until you know him better. Maybe you'll grow to like him, and maybe . . ."

"Adrienne!" I said.

"Okay, okay!" She laughed, and glanced at the door as someone knocked. "Here's Elsa with your things. Elsa, I'll put her clothes away if you will run Fräulein Mitchell's bath."

I sank gratefully onto the edge of my bed and

looked around. A fire burned brightly in the huge open fireplace. The maid had put down my luggage and was opening the door of an *en suite* bathroom off the bedroom. Adrienne was opening another door to disclose a small office complete with typewriter, desk, cupboards, and a shelf of books.

"He's had Herman prepare this suite for you," Adrienne explained. "He said you may have to work here some nights, if you get behind with your work. You'll find everything you need here—encyclopedias, dictionaries, German- and English-language textbooks. You name it and it's here. . . ."

She broke off, called Elsa from the bathroom, and ran to me. I guess the day had caught up with me, for I had collapsed on the big four-poster bed.

I realized vaguely that I was being undressed, sponged with deliciously warm water, and put to bed, and then there was nothing. . . .

★ 3 ★

I awakened in terror with the impressions of last night still upon me. It took time to adjust, to realize I was safe at Valhalla, that it was morning and I was warm and comfortable and there were other women in the room with me. The maid Elsa had lifted the cover from a meal trolley, and a blond woman of about fifty was inspecting the dishes beneath. A door across the room that I hadn't noticed before was open, and I could see Adrienne in her adjoining bedroom moving about in nightgown and robe.

Whatever the maid had in the dishes on her meal trolley smelled delicious. Its fragrance reminded me that I hadn't eaten since lunch at the airport yesterday, and then had only a tuna-salad roll and coffee. I felt so ravenous that I decided I must be healthy this morning, and sat up.

The women both turned, startled, and the blond called to Adrienne, "Nurse Courbet! Your friend is awake!"

Adrienne came hurrying in, but her anxiety changed to a smile when she saw me. "How do you feel, Lorna?"

40

"*Hungry!*"

She laughed and looked at the blond woman, who was crossing the bedroom to join us. "You see, Fräulein Richter? This morning she is okay, as I thought she would be. Last night she was just mentally and physically exhausted. She'll be good as new after she's had breakfast. Lorna, this is Herman's cousin Erma Richter. She insisted we have the family doctor look at you this afternoon when he calls to see Herr Richter."

The woman nodded to me stiffly. "Fräulein!"

She had the cold blue eyes of Paul, the same strongly chiseled features and athletic body. But she could smile, I saw, and the smile changed her, making her seem more human.

"I still think Dr. Brewster should see you, Fräulein Mitchell," she said pleasantly enough. "Since he is making his regular call upon my uncle in any case, why not? I have seen more of such things than Nurse Courbet. Last night you were not dressed for our winter, and I have seen what frostbite can lead to. Gangrene is not a pleasant thing to have, I assure you."

I glanced at Adrienne uncertainly, and she shrugged and smiled. "Very well, Fräulein Richter, I'll make sure she sees Dr. Brewster," Adrienne said in a conciliatory tone. "Now, if you don't mind, I'll see that she has her breakfast. Dr. Brewster never gets here before noon, and Herr Richter never works on Sunday, so she can rest until then."

The blond woman nodded. "I hope you have no further trouble, Fräulein Mitchell. I notice the hyperemia seems less in your fingers this morning. A good sign. I can't imagine what Paul could have been thinking last night, to leave you alone on that road in an open jeep."

"It has canvas curtains, Fräulein," Adrienne reminded her acidly. "And your cousin only left her to bring a fresh battery."

"Canvas curtains? The girl is lucky she's alive!" She had reddened angrily. She inclined her head toward the door, and the maid followed her out.

"Erma never can forget that she was a nurse in Europe in World War Two," Adrienne said resentfully when she had gone. "Anyhow, she only had two years' nursing, then the war ended. The family took her with them to Spain in 1945, Herman says."

"She seemed to want to help me," I said apologetically in Fräulein Richter's defense.

Adrienne sniffed. "You're lucky she didn't treat your frostbite last night. In her day they probably used to rub the reddened part with snow. I treated you with warmth. There are three degrees of frostbite, and yours was only first degree. You had hyperemia last night, caused by blood gathering in the affected part, reddening the skin. Your hyperemia is just about gone this morning. Now, how about breakfast? I had mine sent up so we could breakfast together. You are free all day, the old man never works on Sunday. You don't have to worry about a thing, just rest and settle in. Okay?"

I smiled. "Sounds great!" I sniffed hungrily at

the steaming food. In the bathroom, someone had set out fresh towels and soap.

"Don't hurry," she called after me. "I can keep breakfast hot on the trolley."

"We live in luxury?" That had been a standing joke between us once, traveling as *au pair* girls, often working for just hard beds and skimpy meals.

"You don't know the half of it!" she said.

We breakfasted in front of the fire in our robes and nightgowns, and the breakfast was delicious. Erma Richter, I learned, was the Valhalla housekeeper, and even Adrienne, who didn't like her, agreed that she kept the house immaculate and hadn't served a poor meal since the family came to America. Erma was fifty and had never married; she had devoted herself to her uncle's family.

We finished breakfast, and a different maid wheeled the trolley out and came back later to make the beds and tidy up. The interruption moved us into my study, where we talked on and on. I would not have believed two people could find so much to talk about—both past and present.

In the quiet sanctuary of the study she told me that Johann Richter was a former wartime industrialist who was accused of being a war criminal at the Nuremberg trials following World War Two. But Johann, she assured me, was completely exonerated from charges that the chemicals and gases manufactured by the Richter corporation were lethal and had been used to kill innocent people. If he hadn't been completely and unequivocally exonerated, he would never have been allowed to come to America to live.

"I've never believed that old man could do anything like that," she told me confidentially. "And neither will you when you get to know him. But he did have close business relations with some of the Nazi leaders, and this meant he had to mix with them socially. That was the way they were. Herman says Johann admitted this freely at the trials. . . ."

I frowned. "I suppose this is what the memoirs are all about?"

"I believe the memoirs mean more to the poor old man than anything else in his life. Herman says he has always been very bitter about being brought to trial, when he knew he was innocent. Herman believes, and so do I, that he is only writing his memoirs in an attempt to clear himself once and for all of any stigma remaining from the trial. Paul has been against the writing of the memoirs from the beginning. Paul is very bitter about it."

"And Herman?"

"Herman is worried about it too, but not in the same way Paul is," Adrienne said. "I mean, Herman isn't *bitter* about it. But he is very worried about what his father might write."

"I don't see what either of them has to worry about," I puzzled. "He was exonerated, you say, and he's here. How can the memoirs harm his sons? What exactly is he writing that could do that?"

She shook her head, frowning. "That's just it.

Nobody knows, including Herman and Paul. We all know he's writing his memoirs, has been working on them for five years now. We all know he was a very important figure in Germany during the war. But only Johann knows what he's writing about."

"His previous secretary would know."

She smiled. "He had secretaries in Germany of course, at the Richter Corporation head office in Stuttgart before he resigned from the presidency of the corporation to write his memoirs, but none since. You are the first person other than Johann who will see them. Nobody knows what he's written, except Johann. Paul and Herman would find out if they could, but that's impossible."

"How is it impossible?" I asked, frowning.

She laughed. "You'll learn all about Johann's security precautions before you start work tomorrow, Lorna. I'm glad I'm just the nurse and you are the secretary! But never mind, maybe he'll make us both immortal by mentioning us in his memoirs. You for putting his words of wisdom on paper for posterity to read, and me for making that possible by keeping him alive to do it."

She broke off; someone had tapped at the study door, and the maid looked in. She glanced at my nightgown and robe, her smile slightly malicious, as Adrienne asked her crisply, "What is it, Marlene?"

"Herr Richter is at the door. He asks may he speak to Fräulein Mitchell."

"Of course," Adrienne said. "Bring him here."

"But . . ." I looked down in dismay at my night clothing, but Adrienne smiled.

"He probably expects to see you in bed, and all he will want to know is if you will be fit for work tomorrow. He won't stare, he's not like that."

It was too late to protest in any case; the maid Marlene was opening the door again. "Herr Richter *Senior*, Fräuleins," she said with emphasis, lest there be any doubt.

I gathered my robe around me defensively as he came in, but after the first glance he did not seem to notice what I wore.

"I hope you are feeling better this morning, Fräulein Mitchell?" The emaciation of his once-strong body was more evident standing. The gaunt, lined face had an unnatural pallor.

"Much better, thank you, Herr Richter." I smiled. "Won't you sit down?"

He shook his head. "Sunday is my rest day, but I felt I should see you before I go to my room for the day. My niece Erma has arranged for Dr. Brewster to see you this afternoon. With frostbite it is as well to be sure. You have no duties today, Fräulein, but tomorrow I will expect you to report to me for work in my study at seven-thirty A.M."

"I will be there, Herr Richter."

"You must be prepared to work late at night, when my health permits."

"I understand that, Herr Richter."

"I hope you will be happy here." He started to turn away, but stopped to look back at me. "If I expect you to work hard, Fräulein, it is because this is made necessary by a deadline I have been told I must meet six months from now." His smile was a grim and twisted caricature of humor, as he added, "A deadline of which I'm sure your friend Nurse Courbet has already informed you."

Sympathy touched me. "I understand your reasons, Herr Richter, and I will do the best I can to help you complete the manuscript."

"Good!" His face seemed calmer, more composed suddenly. "Then tomorrow morning you and I go to work."

"Well!" Adrienne said when he had gone. "He actually smiled. What have you got that I haven't? He's never smiled at me yet."

"I don't have to feed him medicine or give him shots," I said. "A secretary has the advantage over a nurse there."

"Nevertheless, I'm glad I'm the nurse," she said. "I know Herman would give anything to know what his father is writing. And Paul's need must be greater than his. Herman is only thirty-five, but Paul served in the war. And it has just occurred to me that you are going to be the only person other than the old man who will know what he writes. That's going to put you under a lot of pressure from his sons, and probably Erma too."

"But wasn't Paul conscripted? What could he have to fear from what his father writes? Or Herman, or Erma?"

She glanced uneasily at the door. "They seem to fear what the old man may write about himself, Lorna. Herman says his father manufactured top-secret chemicals and gases that could have been used in chemical warfare, even though in fact they never were. And he admits he associated with top Nazi leaders. He had to, of course, and although the poisons were never used and he was exonerated at Nuremberg, suppose Johann writes about these things? Suppose he mentions something that wasn't brought up at the trial—something incriminating?"

I frowned. "What could they do to him?"

"Nothing," she said. "Since Johann is a dying man. But what about the others? Herman likes it here. We have all sorts of plans for when we marry, and being deported has no part in them, believe me."

I shook my head. "These things are hypothetical. Johann may never have done anything wrong. Courts like Nuremberg don't exonerate accused men without good reason." And the more I thought about it, the more positive I became. "If the memoirs serve any purpose for Johann Richter, Adrienne," I told her, "it can only be to prove the judgment given then to be a wise and correct decision. If he was responsible for something criminal, why would he want to make it public, even after his death, when it would hurt his family?"

Adrienne lowered her voice and glanced at the closed door again. "When you work with Johann, you'll know, Lorna," she whispered. "Will you do something for me? Will you put Herman's mind at rest? And Paul's? Because anything that hurts

Paul must harm Herman too in this thing." She was pleading with me. "Lorna, I love Herman!"

"Suppose he, *Johann* . . . asks me not to reveal what I read to anyone?"

Momentarily she looked horrified. "What makes you think he might do so?"

"If it's so important to him, why not expect his secretary to keep it secret?"

She stared at me angrily. "Could you keep a promise like that? When you know that our happiness depends upon our knowing?"

I shook my head uneasily. How could I answer that? "I can't tell you, Adrienne," I muttered. "I don't know what I would do. We're talking about a hypothetical situation that may never arise."

"As his brain deteriorates, he could write anything," she said. "I think it's that, and just not knowing, that worry Herman and Paul most." She shook her head, close to the tears she had always seemed able to summon effortlessly when necessary. "I thought you were my friend, Lorna," she told me piteously.

"I won't hurt you, if I can avoid it. I shouldn't need to tell you that, Adrienne."

"Then you'll reconsider?"

"Let's just not talk about it today. Okay?"

She looked contrite. "Darling, I'm sorry! This thing is so important to me, so important to Herman's and my future life together, that I can't think of anything else. I'm forgetting the terrible experience you had last night. I'm sorry, Lorna. I promise, I won't mention it again today."

And Paul Richter was responsible for that terrifying ordeal, I remembered bitterly. "I'm still trying to forget last night, Adrienne," I said.

"I still think you should keep an open mind about Paul until you know him better," she said. "He was doing what he considered best to get you out of trouble, I'm sure. And he can be awfully nice. Now, if you'd only forget what happened and be nice to him, he'd respond. You and I might even become sisters-in-law one day, with wealthy husbands, too—and I mean wealthy!"

"No way, Adrienne!" I said grimly. "I told you, I don't like the guy."

"Okay," she said, shrugging slim shoulders. "Miss the chance of a lifetime, the sort of chance other girls dream about, if you want to. Who cares? It's your loss."

She seemed so annoyed with what she considered my foolishness that I had to giggle, and though at first she looked surprised, in a moment she was smiling too.

"I should know better than try to find a boyfriend for you!" She laughed.

"You *should* know better!" I agreed.

"Remember that time in Rouen when I arranged a blind date for you and finished up stuck with them both just because you didn't like the way the guy looked at you?"

"He looked at me like a lascivious satyr," I remembered indignantly.

"So what guy's perfect?" she said. "I'll tell you one thing, Lorna—there's not much choice at Valhalla. It's Herman or Paul. And don't you dare look at Herman—he's mine."

"There must be guys in the village."

"Nobody you would look at," she said with certainty.

I laughed. "Really? Do you know an artist who stays at the widow Clout's place?"

Mentally, as I said it, I found myself comparing the young man I'd met so briefly in the village with Paul Richter. Paul, I acknowledged, just didn't compare. I admitted that was probably because other than Adrienne's, Rick Byron's was the only really friendly face I'd seen since I left California.

"Well? Don't you know him?" I asked her calmly, when she didn't answer.

"Of course I know him!" she said. "I was wondering how it is that you do, that's all. And why, if you do, you didn't mention him before. But maybe we're not talking about the same guy. What's he like, this man you met?"

"There was a blackout in the village, so how would I know what he looks like? I barely noticed. But he was nice to me, and his name is Rick Byron. They . . . he and the storekeeper, Mr. Harkness, expected me to be stranded in the village. Rick was taking me to the widow Clout's place to stay overnight when we saw the lights of Paul's jeep coming. I only mentioned him because you seem to think there are no other guys here than Paul and Herman Richter. You're wrong, you know, Adrienne."

"But surely you can't compare him with Paul?"

"Oh, but I can," I said. "I like men with dark hair and smiling gray eyes. I thought he was much better-looking than Paul, and he's certainly much more polite. Rick Byron was nice to me. I like him. I can't say the same of Paul Richter. Could you call Paul kind, thoughtful, sensitive?"

She sniffed. "You have to give Paul a chance. You got off to a bad start with him. So you barely noticed Rick Byron? You saw him for a few minutes in a storm with Fifeness blacked out? Now you tell me he's more handsome than Paul. You tell me he has black hair and smiling gray eyes; that he's polite, thoughtful, sensitive, and he seemed very nice to you?"

"Don't you like Rick Byron?" I asked her resentfully.

"Like him?" she said. "Really, Lorna, I hardly know him. And neither do you, if you ask me. Maybe you'd better give yourself a chance to see him in daylight before you start imagining him as some sort of Prince Charming. And get to know them both before you start making judgments."

"Oh, I mean to see him again," I said. "If only to thank him for his help last night. Paul, by the way, went out of his way to insult him." And that, I decided now, was another reason for me to dislike Paul Richter.

She shrugged. "You'll do what you want, as always," she said. "You'll find Rick Byron any day, once the weather breaks. You'll see him along the clifftops or in the village with his paints, brushes, and easel. He paints seascapes and fishing boats and stuff like that. You can find him easily enough if ever you want to see him." She shook her head, studying me. "Sometimes I just don't understand you, Lorna! He isn't even a good artist, Herman says."

"Paul thinks the same. However, Herr Richter Senior must disagree. And by the way, Adrienne, I don't have to look for Rick along the clifftops. He's coming here to Valhalla to paint Herr Richter's portrait for the book cover. Didn't you know that either? Herr Richter has already commissioned him to paint the portrait."

She was staring at me in astonishment. "Does Paul know this?"

"When he tried to tell me, as you said Herman told you, that Rick's work showed no talent, I said that seemed strange to me because Herr Richter, his own father, had commissioned Rick to paint his portrait."

She shook her head. "You went out of your way to antagonize Paul? Lorna, was that wise when you were coming here to work?"

"There are some things a girl just has to say."

"Some girls," she retorted. "And, Lorna, you can forget that guy from the village, and the sooner the better. He's far too busy with his work to look at girls, whether he has talent or he doesn't. Even a girl as attractive as you are. The sea and the cliffs, the fishing boats and the gulls, are all Rick Byron ever sees."

"Want to bet?" I asked her.

She laughed, and as always, I found her laughter contagious. I never could be angry with her for long, so I laughed too. We returned to reminiscences and safer ground by mutual consent.

Adrienne did not come down for lunch. Dr.

Brewster arrived early, and she was in Johann's room attending her patient and the doctor. For luncheon companions I had Paul, Herman, and Erma. The food was, Erma informed me, one of her special family meals from recipes she used in Germany before the Richter family came to America.

The food was great, but heavy, Holstein Schnitzels, which Adrienne had told Erma were a favorite dish of mine, and later the maids served delicious Lübeck marzipan pastry. Sipping coffee, I wondered why Adrienne hadn't put on more weight. She must really be interested in Herman Richter, I decided, and staying slim to look her best. In Europe she had been inclined to put on weight quickly when the food was good. I was going to have to watch my weight, if today's lunch was typical of Erma Richter's meals.

The men ate wolfishly. They were both big men, and both overweight by American standards. In Germany it hadn't seemed to matter so much to women if their men were not streamlined athletic types. Adrienne and I had supposed that was an aftermath of the war and wartime rationing. I liked Herman the better of Johann Richter's sons. He was younger and more pleasant than Paul, and I could understand Adrienne falling for him.

Herman, with his black hair and brown eyes, seemed Paul's opposite in many ways. He could be entertaining, and several times during lunch I laughed as he described the early problems of the family newly arrived in America. Even Erma smiled at the memories. But Paul listened silently, his stern face grim, his blue eyes cold and hostile, remembering only what he considered insults. Herman could laugh at himself and the mistakes his family had made then, but Paul could not. That, I decided, epitomized the difference in the brothers.

We were dawdling over coffee when Adrienne came in. She had time for only a cup of coffee, she told Erma, then she would take one back for Dr. Brewster. When Herman asked her how his father was, she said Dr. Brewster was worried about his condition and wanted him to rest on Monday. But Johann had refused. He was eager to start work with me on the typing and translation of his manuscript.

The maid brought Adrienne Dr. Brewster's coffee, and she glanced at the clock. "Dr. Brewster will see you at two-thirty, Lorna," she said. "He expects to be finished with Herr Richter about then. He'll see you in your room. Okay?"

I nodded reluctantly. I had forgotten Erma had arranged for the doctor to see me, but Erma had not, for she was smiling, pleased.

"I meant to show you Valhalla today, Lorna," Adrienne said disappointedly. "Paul, what are you doing this afternoon?"

Paul Richter glanced up quickly. "In this weather? Why ask, Fräulein? I'd be delighted to show Fräulein Mitchell around. I'd like to make up for the bad impression I gave her at our first meeting. Have you shown her the greenhouses yet? In weather like this, they are the only things here worth seeing, in my opinion."

"I thought I'd write some letters . . ." I began to say. But they both ignored me as though I hadn't spoken.

"Then that's settled," Adrienne said decisively. "Lorna, you'll really enjoy seeing the greenhouses. They're Herr Richter's hobby, when he isn't writing memoirs. He planned and stocked them with flowers, but the electronic engineering is Paul's. Paul can show you the greenhouses and give you a better explanation of how things work than anyone else. You're lucky Paul's available."

"I don't doubt it, but my letters . . ."

I had never seen Paul Richter smile before. He was handsome, I realized, surprised.

"Please, Fräulein?" he said. "Let me make up for the fright I gave you—even though unintentional—last night?"

He seemed sincere, I decided. And I didn't want to antagonize him any further. If I was to work and live here at Valhalla, having Paul Richter for my enemy could make my life very difficult. He was too full of anger and arrogance. A man like that could be dangerous.

I nodded, and managed a weak smile. "But I have an appointment with Dr. Brewster."

"At two-thirty, Paul!" Adrienne reminded him, smiling triumphantly. "Have her upstairs by two-thirty."

"I promise," he said, smiling back at her.

"Will I need warmer clothes? Are the greenhouses far from the house?" I asked nervously as Adrienne went out with Dr. Brewster's coffee.

Paul laughed. "No, of course not, Fräulein. I

had a covered walk constructed to the green-houses. Heated, like the greenhouses themselves. Come as you are." His eyes studied me admiringly. "Come just as you are."

Adrienne's laughter sounded mischievously as she went out. "Have fun, Lorna!" she said.

★ 4 ★

"This is the door normally used to enter the covered way from the house," Paul Richter informed me as we stopped at a door in the passage on the north side of Valhalla. I stared around curiously but could see only closed doors, and this was a wing of the great house that I hadn't seen before.

"The greenhouses are through there?" There was nothing to be seen except a closed door which appeared sealed with rubber flaps that covered the cracks around the door.

"They are not really greenhouses," he corrected me. "Hothouses. The hothouse's function is different from that of a greenhouse. Literally, the greenhouse is for the shelter and protection of tender plants. These hothouses are for growing tropical plants which must be kept at a high temperature at all seasons here in Maine."

"What are the rubber seals around the edges of the door for, Herr Richter?"

He smiled. "You are observant, Fräulein. The seals are designed in part to keep the hot air from escaping. But tropical plants like any others are susceptible to disease and infestation by fungus, parasites, and insects. Since our rare plants would have no resistance to the local pests, these must be destroyed when they appear inside the hothouses. We must spray with insecticides which might irritate or even be quite harmful to people in the house. The rubber seals prevent that in the same way they prevent the escape of the warmth from inside."

"The seals are your idea?"

He nodded. "As Adrienne said, the flowers are my father's, but the engineering is mine. Without my help I doubt that he would have grown one bloom in there. He is a dreamer, my father. A planner. Such people will never realize or admit that without men like me, willing and able to carry out the hard, sometimes dangerous, and often unpleasant task of creating the reality, their dreams would amount to nothing."

He said it with so much vehemence that I wondered if he meant the hothouses at all. Or something bigger; something more disturbing to him and to Johann Richter, his father?

"Yet the plan must be created before the hard work of building the reality can begin. Isn't that so, Herr Richter?"

He shrugged, and changed the subject, turning away from the rubber-sealed door. "We will need light to see the flowers. The master controls are farther along the passage in another room." He gave me a sidelong glance. "The beauty of flowers, I have to confess, holds little attraction for me. I would sooner admire a lovely woman. But give me a problem in chemistry or engineering or electronics that is a challenge, and I will work at it day and night. So my father has his rare plants, and I have something to keep me busy and interested in this benighted place. There is always some new problem occurring in the hothouses. This, I like."

"Then it is good for you both." I smiled.

"Yes." He had stopped at a door, securely locked, for it took him time to open it, and when he did, an alarm sounded somewhere inside. He went in quickly to turn it off. Following him, I stared around curiously. I was standing in what appeared to be a well-equipped scientific laboratory. A bank of electronic equipment lined one wall. Test tubes and chemicals were stored neatly on the shelves or were being used in current experiments on laboratory benches. Seeds, leaves, and mold were being examined.

"You find my den interesting?" He had returned from the control panel of the alarm and was studying my face, his expression amused.

"It looks more like a scientist's laboratory than a den to me, Herr Richter."

"Would you be surprised if I told you that you are the only other human being who has entered here since I had the room constructed?"

"I would be surprised, yes." I laughed. "And flattered. What are you creating in here—an atom bomb?"

He frowned. "Nothing so lethal, Fräulein. Except, of course, to pests I wish to exterminate so that my father's rare plants can thrive. Most of the experiments you see are set up to study the effects of pesticides on plant viruses. I prefer to make my own pesticides, liquid or gas. I find them much more effective than those they sell here in your country. But no doubt it will be the flowers that interest you, not my experiments. We must have light, and there has been some spray used in the hothouses that must be dispersed."

He moved to the electronic control board. Somewhere a faint humming sound started, and he walked back and closed the outer door of the laboratory. I looked at him suspiciously. He smiled when he saw my expression.

"You still do not trust me, Fräulein? Another door in here leads into the covered way. We do not need to go back into the passage. Are you coming? By the time we reach the hothouse complex, the pesticide my father's gardeners have been using will have completely dispersed. The air in there will be as fresh as you could wish."

"I'm sorry, Herr Richter," I said, remembering. "I suppose I can't forget what happened at the Devil's Bend."

"I was only doing what I thought best for you," he said coldly.

"I know you thought so, Herr Richter," I said quickly. "But I was terrified at the thought of being left alone in that awful place. I didn't realize what you intended when you got out of the jeep. When I called, you didn't seem to hear. You left too quickly for me to tell you how frightened I really was."

Studying my face, he shook his head slowly.

"You called me? You wanted me to come back? I didn't hear you, Fräulein. I most certainly would not have left you there alone if I had known you were so terrified."

I avoided those expressionless blue eyes staring at me; they made me uneasy, brought back a small recurrence of my fear.

"Well, that's over. It doesn't matter now," I muttered uneasily.

"It does to me, if you still think I would deliberately harm you in any way," he said grimly. "If you had stayed in the jeep, you would not have been in any danger. I got back as quickly as I could. I was shocked to find the jeep empty."

"I left it because I was starting to fall asleep. I'd heard before that feeling drowsy and insensible to the cold as I did was a prelude to death by freezing."

"People exaggerate these things," he said, frowning.

"And there was something else, too. Only . . ."

"Only what, Fräulein?" His blue eyes hardened, seeking some motive in what I said.

"I saw someone coming. Walking. Not from where I thought you disappeared, but from the direction of the village."

"Impossible!" he said.

"I saw someone, Herr Richter! I called to him, thinking it was you returning."

"The turnoff to the chauffeur's house is in the other direction," he said. "Toward Valhalla. There's a break in the cliff there, a sidetrack." He shook his head. "Nobody would come that way last night, not walking. You saw a shadow, Fräulein. You were scared because of my . . . my mistake in leaving you alone. Your imagination did the rest."

"It was no shadow I saw, Herr Richter," I said. "It was a man. I called to him, asking if it was you, but he wouldn't answer. So I ran."

"When people run from danger, cowardice increases their fear," he said. "You saw shadows, unless you can believe, as the ignorant folk in Fifeness village do, that the Devil's Bend is haunted by the ghosts of people who drowned in the sea at the foot of the cliff. As you could have drowned because you left the jeep."

"I saw a man, Herr Richter," I said stubbornly. "When I turned to run from him, I slipped and fell, and he almost caught me. But in his eagerness he slipped and fell too, so I got away. I saw the break in the cliff, and decided that was the way you had gone to the chauffeur's house. He chased me to the side road, then stopped as though he wasn't sure which way I had gone. But by then I could see the lights of this house, and the road ahead was more sheltered."

He frowned at me. "If he had gone toward the Connell house, I would have met him."

"Perhaps he turned back because he thought I fell. When I turned the Devil's Bend the wind knocked me down. But I was blown back against the cliff wall. I managed to creep along the rock wall and didn't see him again until I rounded the next corner and reached the break in the cliff."

"Why would he follow you there if he thought you fell at the Devil's Bend?" he demanded.

"He could have been checking, thinking I had fallen, but wanting to make sure."

He was scowling at me suspiciously. "You seem so sure that you saw a man. Yet what you say is impossible. You have me confused, Fräulein. I do not know what to think. You do not by any chance suspect that the man you think you saw was me?"

"Naturally I thought it was you, at first. Until I called to him asking if it was you and he did not answer. It was then I became afraid. It was then that I ran away . . . and was almost killed."

"If you had called to me as I returned with the battery, I would have answered. In any case, I would have come from the opposite direction. From the Connell house. Do you accept that now?"

I smiled. "Yes, of course. But if it was not you, who was it?"

He shrugged. "Who knows, if what you saw really was a man? It would have to be some vagrant, some stranger to the district, who had wandered onto the cliff road by mistake. Who perhaps saw the abandoned jeep and was tempted to steal it. Or worse. I am sure of one thing, Fräulein. No local man would have been walking that road last night. But I promised to show you the hothouses, not remind you of unpleasant things. The door is at the end of the laboratory. Coming?"

He was opening the door politely for me; electronically controlled lights automatically flicked on as the door opened.

I smiled. "Another of your ideas, Herr Richter?" I inquired.

"One of many," he said.

I followed him out into a covered passage where glass roof and walls gleamed in the light, reflected from some stronger material sheathing and protecting it from the weather outside. The outer covering looked like aluminum, I decided. It was pleasantly warm in the passage. The door of the laboratory closed automatically behind us.

He glanced up at the roof. "This is another idea of mine. No glass house could stand against the winter weather here without protection. Gale-force winds are common hereabouts, and at times we have sleet almost as large as your hailstones in California. And of course debris of all kinds is carried on winds like the present one. Yet in summertime we have sunshine that the plants need."

"So what did you do?"

"What you see through the glass is a strong and durable sheath of aluminum. It forms a protective skin, electronically controlled, that can be rolled back at the touch of a switch when there is sunlight. Or in bad weather such as we have now, can fully protect the glass. It would take a very heavy blow to dent the aluminum enough to break the glass. Even then, probably only one pane would be shattered, the one at the point of impact."

"The hothouses are sheathed in the same way?"

"Exactly. The sheathing there retracts in the same manner. The aluminum protecting the walls retracts up under the eaves. The roof sheathing on each sloping side retracts up to the central ridgepole, allowing the sunlight full access except for a two-foot width of rolled aluminum."

"It sounds ingenious."

"I'd demonstrate it for you, except that the risk of damage would be too great just now. It's still blowing a full gale outside. Hear *that*?"

Something had struck the aluminum sheathing heavily. I heard it grate as it slid down the roof and fell. I shivered, remembering last night. The wind had seemed less this morning in the great house, but here, with only glass and aluminum around us, the sounds of the storm were almost as bad as yesterday.

"There's no need to be nervous," he said reassuringly. "The house protects us from the worst of the prevailing wind. The noise may be worse, but noise isn't going to hurt you."

"I'm not scared," I lied.

We were almost at the end of the covered way. I expected to see the colorful display of the first hothouse through glass, but ahead was just an aluminum wall with a closed central door. He smiled at my expression.

"My father likes to surprise the few people he ever brings here," he said. "He believes, and I'm inclined to agree with him, that your first glimpse of his flowers blooming as they are now will be the one you are most likely to remember. Walk ahead to the door, and you will understand what he means."

"But . . ." I glanced at him suspiciously.

"Just trust me for once and do as I say, Fräulein. I promise you won't regret it."

"Well . . ." I laughed nervously, and obeyed, walking ahead uneasily, aware of his nearness as he followed. "How do you open the door?" I asked. "It has no handle."

"Don't tell me you haven't seen doors that open electronically in California?"

I should have known! I stepped forward onto the metal mat that triggered the device. The doors began to part smoothly, and I gasped in delight. It was as though the curtains of a theater were opening to display the banks of glorious flowers within, growing tier on tier to a central high point. It was like entering a tropical wonderland of the most glorious begonias, cyclamen, and other exotic blooms that I had ever seen. To me each bloom seemed a perfect specimen of its kind, and when I remembered the bleak winter landscape outside, the contrast amazed me.

The magnificent butterfly-shaped flowers of the cyclamen were massed in what seemed every possible color—pink, red, salmon, lilac, mauve; I stared at them enthralled. The tiers of tuberous begonias rose above them, even more glorious in shape and color. And on either side of this splendid display, benches of superb potted liliums lined the walls or trailed from hanging baskets attached to hooks on the roof supports.

Light flooded the hothouse, reflecting from the glass, and the whole effect of blazing and unexpected color both awed and delighted me.

"Well?" Paul Richter's impatient voice brought me back reluctantly from what seemed perfection.

"I don't have words to describe it! They're the

most beautiful collection of flowers I've ever seen."

"There are three hothouses like these. His collection should be world-famous, but he is more interested in his stupid memoirs."

"If they can take your father away from enjoyment of this, they must be important to him." I was moving admiringly along the narrow walk between the central tiers and the benches of graceful liliums along the wall.

"They are not important—they are a mistake!" he said angrily. "The past is dead and buried. Why exhume it now that he is dying? Your friend Adrienne has told you this, surely? That he has a brain tumor that is killing him?"

"Yes."

"How can a man of his age, when even in good health he must be senile, write the unbiased truth? He is eighty years old. And to make the project he attempts utterly impossible, he has an incurable and inoperable illness affecting his brain. Who knows what he writes? He tells us, his only relatives, nothing. He has withdrawn from us. He locks himself in his study. He will tell us nothing. Yet what he is writing can harm the whole family collectively and individually."

I came back to him slowly between the banked flowers. "The liliums are magnificent, aren't they?" I said, trying to distract him. He did not answer. His bulk barred my way on the narrow walk. His blue eyes were angry with me.

"It is this not knowing what he writes that makes me bitter, Fräulein," he muttered. "You could help us if you would. Help *us*, for it is not for myself alone that I ask. If in his state of health he confuses fact with fantasy, he may harm us all, including your friend Adrienne Courbet, who loves my brother, Herman."

"I told you how I felt about this on the cliff road, Herr Richter," I muttered, moving back from him a little.

"I haven't forgotten. I admire you for the loyalty you expressed. But now that you have seen him, you must realize that what I said is true. He is not capable of writing factually. He is a sick man, a dying man."

"Whatever it is you fear he may write, Herr Richter, he may never write at all. Even if, as you suspect, his mind is affected. And I have worked for American publishers. I know that they are wary of publishing anything that could be considered defamatory. If, for instance, your father wrote something accusing you, they would not publish it unless they were sure they could prove that what he had written was the truth, and its publication was in the public interest."

"Words!" he growled. "You are good at words, and so is he. Words can be twisted to entangle anyone."

"Have you tried asking your father to allow you to check for accuracy the facts he is writing about?"

"And demanded the right to do that in the family interest," he said bitterly. "Only to be told that what he writes is his memoirs, not mine, and to be reminded that he is still the head of this house while he lives."

"The suggestion angered him?"

"He is a man easily angered."

Like you, I thought. I said, "But you are his son, surely he would not harm you."

"I would hope not. I have been a good son to him. So has Herman, and Erma has served him patiently all her life. Yet, how does one know, the way he is now?"

I shrugged. "I have met your father only briefly, Herr Richter." I glanced at my wristwatch. "Are there more hothouses to see, or shall we go back?"

"There are others," he said reluctantly. "There will be people working in there, no doubt. The display will not be quite like this. But come, you have time."

I followed as he turned in the narrow way. On the other side of the central tiers we walked past pots of African violets along the wall. Exotic red lilies, others with highly perfumed green bracts.

Another wall of aluminum separated the first hothouse from the next. It opened in the same way to disclose banks of tiered ferns of all descriptions. Trailers of flowers hung from baskets suspended from the roof frame, but the color of the first spectacular hothouse was missing. Two men working among the pots glanced up and smiled.

"Guten Tag, Fräulein!" one said politely. The other nodded.

I made some comment on the ferns, and we moved on. "The staff are all German, Herr Richter?"

"My father insists that only German is spoken here," he said. "Most of our people migrated with us from Germany. But not all. Adrienne, for instance, is French, and you are American. The chauffeur, Connell, is an American; he was a prisoner of war and learned to speak German in some stalag in Germany."

Entering the third and last hothouse, I wondered if Johann Richter had broken his German-speaking rule in the case of Rick Byron. But remembering how Paul Richter felt about the artist, I did not ask.

"They are potting in here, and there has been spraying," he said as I looked around. "There is not so much to see here. When the plants in the first hothouse have bloomed, they are brought in here. Their place is continually being taken by other flowers coming into full bloom. The hothouses are constantly in a state of flux. Since the ferns do not have showy blooms, the traffic is all between houses one and three. As you see, there are plenty of buds in here, but few flowers. This is where most of the work is done."

"Other greenhouses I've seen have a connecting passage. Why do these open directly into each other?"

He nodded approvingly. "A good question, Fräulein. The whole complex constructed this way can be turned into one huge hothouse having full benefit of the light and sun in the summer months. The transition is made electronically, of course. Controls are in the fourth building of the complex, and the lab. Let me demonstrate."

I followed him past where two men and a young woman were potting plants with warm earth from which steam arose. The door at the end of the third hothouse opened as we stepped on its mat, disclosing the fourth building, full of workbenches, stored earth and fertilizer, empty pots, and tools. It was almost unpleasantly warm inside.

"You notice it is warmer?" he asked. "There is some fermentation in here that increases the temperature." He began to open the cover of a switchboard on the wall. "No glass walls in here, just metal," he added. "And of course all power and electronic equipment in here can be monitored and adjusted, switched on or off at will from the master panel in my laboratory. Now, watch."

He chose a switch; then something clicked and began to whir faintly. The twin doors at the end of the workroom where we stood were parting as though someone had stepped on the opening device. But there was a difference, I saw; the crack where the doors parted was opening right up to the ridgepole of the buildings. It was opening in two parts, the aluminum folding upon itself in a concertina action.

The workers were looking up, surprised, from where they worked. The doors and walls between the other hothouses were folding back in the same controlled way. I could see the blaze of color of the magnificent flowers in the first hothouse at the end of what had become a long hall of glass enclosed by the outer metal sheathing.

"You could hold a ball in here, Herr Richter!"
I murmured, awed.

"The thought has occurred to me," he said with
a hint of amusement. "On a starlight night with
the metal sheathing back, this place is beautiful."

"Like the ballroom in the Cinderella fairy
tale!"

He smiled. "What a romantic you are,
Fräulein!" he said. "Yes, it could be like that, except that we do not have enough friends in this
country to fill one corner of one hothouse—certainly not three."

"Whose fault is that?" I remembered what he
had said when we met, and could not resist adding: "When you told me you consider the people of
Fifeness ignorant peasants?"

"As they consider us foreigners and intruders,"
he retorted. He glanced at his watch. "But I must
return you to the house as promised. There is just
time." He stood politely aside for me to pass. "I
hope I didn't bore you with the mechanics of this
place. But as I told you, only the flowers belong to
my father. The rest is mine."

"I thought the flowers you showed me in the
first hothouse were the most beautiful sight I have
ever seen," I said appreciatively. "And without
your ingenuity that would not have been possible,
you said. So how could I be bored by the mechanics that made this possible?"

He smiled, pleased. "This is true," he said, as
eagerly as though he needed my approval. "Glass
is necessary to conserve heat and light, but glass as
protective covering is too fragile. Here, where the

winds are so strong in winter, it is useless, but the sheathing is not the only reason why my father's flowers could never bloom as they do without my help. They need the pesticides and special fertilizers I make for them in my laboratory. There is more to producing showy blooms than putting plants in pots, Fräulein."

"As your gardeners do?"

"Yes. The soils used must be continually tested. Nutrient trace elements lacking must be added if the species requires. The requirements of each variety of plant can be different. I study these things in the laboratory and supply the answers and the elements. The people you see in here merely have to follow my instructions, using the materials I supply to promote growth, cure disease, or eradicate the pest."

We had reached the first hothouse, and the glorious blooms held me silent until we reached the passage. I allowed my breath to sigh out contentedly. "Wonderful! Surely you can both be proud of that?"

He smiled. "Proud? In a way, I suppose I am, though I would not admit this to everyone, Fräulein. I feel pride that the blooms are large, the colors right, that parasites or molds have not marked the leaves or deformed the blooms."

We had reached the passage; the door of the laboratory opened soundlessly as we reached it, and closed again behind us.

"Am I late for my appointment with Dr. Brewster?"

He glanced at his watch. "You have plenty of

time. You will find it cold upstairs after the temperature in here. Would you care for a drink, something warming to fortify you against the change in temperature?"

"No, thanks, Herr Richter. If you don't mind, I'll go back to my room and change before I see Dr. Brewster."

"You look quite charming the way you are," he said gruffly. "There is a clock on the wall above my desk, and I guarantee it accurate to the second. I would not have it any other way. If you will not join me in a drink, stay with me until I drink mine, and we cân walk back together. You might become lost in Valhalla."

I laughed. "You're joking!"

"I don't want you to run away from me like you did last night. Agreed?"

I glanced at the clock, and saw I had a good quarter of an hour. "Well, okay, but don't take too long over your drink, Herr Richter."

"Stop calling me that," he said. "You don't have to be deferential to me—you are not a servant. My name is Paul. When you were in Germany traveling with Adrienne as an *au pair* girl, did you call everyone you stayed with Herr Schmidt, or Herr Richter, or whatever?"

I laughed. "That depended on the host."

"Your friend said you were in Stuttgart at one time. We too had *au pair* girls helping in our home in the bad days following the war. I would like to have known you in Stuttgart when you were there."

I had been about to remind him that in what

most Germans thought of as the bad years following World War Two, I had not yet been born. But he had prevented that.

"*Au pair* girls now are mostly university students." I could not bring myself to call him Paul, but if he noticed, he gave no sign.

He was pouring himself a cognac. He said when he caught me looking at it, "Are you sure I can't tempt you? There is also Coke or dry ginger ale if you prefer to spoil cognac as Americans seem to do."

I smiled. "I'm sure, thank you. I don't wish to breathe cognac on Dr. Brewster. Or your father, if we meet."

"Brewster would never notice, he drinks like a fish!" he said contemptuously. "My father was as bad once. He has nothing against alcohol now, except that he's forbidden to drink it. No doubt when you were traveling in Europe your male hosts told you what an attractive girl you are to lonely men?"

"No. We avoided households of lonely men, singular or plural."

"I am the only lonely man here, Lorna," he said. "And I find you most attractive."

"Thank you," I muttered uneasily. "But I think I should go now. I . . ."

All in one movement he drained the cognac and set the glass down.

I was held fast in his arms before I realized what was happening, his face close to mine, and he was about to kiss me. I tried to free myself but could not.

"I have known many girls," he was whispering. "But none like you, none as young and fresh and beautiful. We can be friends, as close friends as Herman and Adrienne are. Perhaps more than that. I could spend my life with a girl like you. But you must help me, liebling! As your friend would help Herman and me if she could."

His kiss hurt my lips, and I had never felt less receptive. He kissed me again, more deeply, before I could wrench myself away from him. I walked to the door, shaken. The door did not open when I stood on the rubber mat covering the triggering device.

I was aware of fear suddenly, but he merely laughed. "The door will not open for you, liebling," he said. "I alone can open it, or the other door that leads back into the hothouses. I could keep you here as long as I wished. Have you thought that I am much stronger than you, and that this laboratory is soundproof?"

"You say you alone can open the door, Herr Richter?" I said shakily. "Then open it!"

"That name again? Say Paul, liebling! It is not a difficult name to say."

"Open the door . . . *Paul.*"

"We will speak of these things again," he said, as though satisfied. The door was opening silently, smoothly.

I sensed his closeness. He stood behind me, but he did not touch me again. "Thank you for showing me the hothouses," I said with forced calm.

"It is the other that you will remember, not the

stupid flowers," he said with arrogant confidence. "We could have something, you and I. Something that we both need. . . ."

I stepped out into the passage, and the door closed behind me. I walked toward the front of the great house, touching my bruised lips.

★ 5 ★

I barely made my appointment with Dr. Brewster, a gray-haired, plump, and rather pompous doctor of what Adrienne called the "old-fashioned school." She said he reminded her of the local GP in the small town in Provence where she was born. But he examined the parts of me that had been frostbitten and pronounced me quite healthy and ready for work in the morning.

His breath smelled strongly of bourbon, proving Paul Richter right in one thing at least. He was right in another way, too, I realized as the afternoon passed pleasantly for me in Adrienne's company: it was what had happened in the laboratory that I was remembering more than the glorious flowers that were Johann's pride and joy. But I was not remembering in the way I knew Paul Richter had meant. Every time I thought of it, I found myself wanting to wipe his kiss from my lips.

Halfway through the afternoon Adrienne began to fidget and look at the door of my room, where we sat talking.

"So what would you like to do now?" I asked her, smiling.

"We've got six months to talk about Europe. Why don't we go downstairs and join the others?" she suggested, grasping the opportunity I'd given her.

"What others?" I asked suspiciously.

"Herman and I usually have a glass of wine and sit in front of the fire about this time on Sunday afternoons. We listen to music or talk."

I smiled. "Okay, go right ahead. I'll see you at dinner. I have letters to write."

She frowned. "No, you must come too. Paul will be there. You can take Paul off our hands, and—"

"No, thanks!" I said, remembering.

She stared at me. "Something happened in the hothouses? I wondered why you didn't say much about the flowers, when everyone else raves about them. What did he do?"

"Nothing, really."

She shook her head. "Don't try to fool me, Lorna—I know you too well. Something happened. I can tell."

"He tried to kiss me," I said resentfully, remembering.

"So what?" She looked relieved. "Isn't that a natural masculine reaction to you? I've seen that happen, remember. And what do you mean, 'tried'? Didn't you want to be kissed?"

"Not by Paul Richter. No. I've told you what I think of him. He's rude and arrogant and conceited, and . . ."

"You told me that before—except the conceited

part. That's new. Well, did you let him kiss you, or didn't you?"

"I didn't have any choice. We were in the laboratory, and he just . . . Well, he just grabbed me when I didn't expect it."

She giggled at my expression. "That I would have liked to see!"

"I thought you were my friend," I said indignantly.

"I told you he could fall for you, Lorna—and I bet he has," she said triumphantly. "Not every girl gets a chance to win a guy with the money he'll have. Come downstairs with me, and we'll find out. I need someone to take his attention away from Herman and me. Your letters will keep. Please, Lorna?"

"Erma can do that," I said resentfully.

"Erma?" She stared at me. "She's his cousin. And besides, Erma is too busy supervising the Sunday dinner."

"I'm not interested in Paul Richter."

"Oh, come on, Lorna, help a friend, will you? It's quite pleasant downstairs on Sunday afternoons. You'll like it, and Paul can be good company. Let him see you're displeased with him, if you want, I don't mind. Though that will only make him keener. But please take him off our backs like a good girl?"

" 'Displeased' isn't the right word," I said grimly. "And it isn't just because of a kiss—it's because he had the audacity to kiss me! It'll be a long time before I forget what happened on the cliff road. A very long time!"

Adrienne knew me well enough to give up. She left in a huff, and I began to write my letters.

When I came down to dinner, Paul wasn't at the table. Adrienne whispered that he was sulking in his room. But whether he was or not, dinner was more pleasant for his absence, it seemed to me. Later, as we went upstairs to our rooms, she said she was sure he had fallen for me. She said all I had to do was forget my hang-up with what happened on the cliff road and let nature take its course. If I did, I'd be well on the way to becoming one of the wealthiest women in America.

I refused to accept that, and went to bed. Tossing restlessly before I slept, I wondered if her need to know what Johann was writing about, so that she could tell Herman, had anything to do with her attempted matchmaking. I decided that it did. Adrienne had changed. She was no longer the girl I'd known. Something, perhaps her association with the Richters, had changed her. She was more sophisticated, more cynically self-seeking than the girl I'd known in Europe.

There was no way I'd ever fall for Paul Richter. No way. . . .

Sleeping, I dreamed that I was in the jeep stalled near the Devil's Bend again, and the dark figure of a man was creeping toward where I huddled in fright, half frozen. Only, as the figure approached, I seemed to know who the man was. It was Paul Richter! I wakened, shocked and whimpering. I thought of asking Adrienne if she had a sleeping pill, but could not bring myself to wake her.

Afterward, when I calmed, I remembered that there was sometimes truth in dreams like that, prompted by the subconscious. Paul had said that he heard me scream and thought I had been blown from the Devil's Bend. So had the unknown figure stalking me that terrifying night. But if that had been Paul, why hadn't he answered when I called to him? And how could he have got where he was, approaching from where I would least expect it, from the village behind us, when he was supposed to have taken the side road ahead that led to the chauffeur's house?

The more my mind worried at these things, the harder it was to sleep. . . .

I wakened with the dull aftermath of a restless night making my head feel numb and useless on this morning when I wanted most to be alert. It was earlier than I was used to rising, and the blond maid Elsa was pouring coffee for me.

"Time to get up, Fräulein Mitchell," she informed me briskly. "Herr Richter will expect you at his study at seven-thirty. He rarely breakfasts when he is working, but we take him coffee and toast to the study. Fräulein Richter will have your breakfast ready in fifteen minutes. Shall I run a bath for you while you drink your coffee?"

"No, thanks, I'll shower." I looked at Adrienne's door, but it was closed. "Is . . . Fräulein Courbet awake yet?"

"She is in bed, Fräulein. She will have given Herr Richter his tablets before he went downstairs an hour ago. She goes back to sleep afterward and has a late breakfast with Fräulein

Richter. He will not need her again until lunchtime, unless he is taken ill, so she might as well sleep. Shall I wake her for you?"

"No, let her sleep."

The hot, strong black coffee helped me return to something like normalcy. I breakfasted alone with Herman. Erma Richter stayed in the kitchen.

Herman chatted pleasantly while we ate, his dark eyes appraising me. "What did you think of the hothouses, Fräulein? My father is proud of his collection of tropical and semitropical plants."

"The flowers are beautiful, so unexpected in this climate, with almost a blizzard outside even now. I've never seen anything like the color, and each flower is a showpiece."

"I sometimes show them to Adrienne. When my father will give me his key to the door from the passage."

"Your brother took me in through the laboratory."

"Really? Then you're the first one he's ever allowed to do that." His surprise was not as genuine as it should be, I decided. There was a hint of sly knowledge in those dark eyes. Adrienne had told him.

"Not even you, Herr Richter?" I asked.

"The laboratory is to Paul what the study is to my father," he said, shaking his head. "Anyone would think he had some closely guarded secret hidden inside. My father is the same. I don't believe people should keep secrets from their own family, do you?"

"I don't believe they should have the need for secrecy."

He chuckled. "Which is a different thing, Fräulein! Well, I don't care what my brother has to hide in there, if anything. Sometimes I think it is just a place where he can hide and sulk when my father's secrecy about the memoirs worries him too much. I hope Paul was nice to you when he showed you around?"

His eyes said that he knew about that too. Adrienne had told him. "Your brother was a perfect guide in the hothouses," I said.

He left it there, smiling. "Frankly, Lorna, Paul's secrecy about his silly laboratory doesn't worry me as much as my father's secrecy about his memoirs. But no doubt Adrienne has told you how I feel about that?"

Why contradict? "She did say something about that. Yes."

He frowned as though surprised. "What did she say?"

I shrugged. "Frankly, Herr Richter, she asked me to tell her what is in the memoirs, so that she could tell you. She said you needed to know, and that your brother's need was greater than yours."

He shook his head. "My poor loyal little Adrienne," he said softly. "Did she say why Paul's need is greater?"

I smiled. "You know why as well as I do. Paul served in the war. You were far too young to do that."

"Paul was conscripted!" he said indignantly.

"I used that argument."

He scowled at me. "What will you do, Fräulein?" he asked anxiously. "Will you help us? Will you help your friend Adrienne, the girl I want to marry? We could have a good life together here in your country when my father dies. This is what we want—to be together here as man and wife. Is that too much to ask?"

"I can only tell you what I told Adrienne," I said. "If your father thinks it so important not to let his family know what he's writing, it seems to me that he will swear me to secrecy."

"But a promise like that is not binding!"

"It is to me, Herr Richter," I said. I glanced at the clock and got up. "He'll be expecting me. . . ."

"You won't reconsider?" he asked angrily, his previous gentle persuasion gone.

"As I told your brother, an employer has a right to expect loyalty from his secretary. I won't break a promise, if he demands one."

"It never occurred to me that he might do that, Lorna." He had controlled his anger and was persuading me gently again. "But suppose he does not demand secrecy from you. It might not take long to skim through the time from the beginning of 1943 to the end of 1944. If he intends to write anything incriminating himself, we believe it must be in that period."

I said slowly, "I think you worry too much about something hypothetical. It may never happen."

"Or it may," he said grimly. "It's not knowing that worries us."

"Suppose he does write, or has written something . . . incriminating? And you find out. What could you do about it?"

"We could prevent its being published." Momentarily it was as though he sensed my agreement and was carried away in his eagerness to believe what he wanted so badly to believe—that I'd help him.

"How?" I asked suspiciously.

"We'd find a way. Paul would, he's smart. Do you know what your government would do to us if my father confessed to being actively involved with the Nazi hierarchy? They'd deport us, all of us. Erma too. Even the servants we brought from Germany with us would be suspect."

"But surely some of you have become naturalized Americans?"

"None of us."

"If you really want to live here permanently, why not?" I demanded, frowning.

"We decided not to become naturalized when he said he would finish his memoirs and have them published in your country," he said emphatically. "Being naturalized wouldn't help us if he incriminated himself. First they denaturalize you by due process of law, then they deport you. It takes a little longer, that's all. The result is the same, and inevitable. And where could we go, what other country would take us if America deported us?"

"But surely, if you point out these things to your father, he will take you into his confidence about the memoirs? Tell you that you have nothing to fear? Adrienne is his nurse. She says he likes her, and you are his younger son. You had no part in the war. If he did wrong, why should he make you suffer for that? He's your father."

"Don't you think we've tried to find out from him? All three of us? He will not even listen. His will is law in this house, and only his death can change that."

"Then it would do no good if I, a stranger, tried to persuade him?"

"No!" he said, alarmed. "Don't try! That would turn him even more bitterly against us, his sons. You don't know my father."

I glanced at the clock. "I'm sorry, Herman," I said. "I must go."

The study was at the opposite side of the building from the principal rooms of the great house. Adrienne had told me where it was on our floor, but I had not seen it. She said a whole suite of rooms, including Johann Richter's own private rooms, were included in the complex that had a library and the study as part of it. Adrienne had said the complex was self-contained, with access by a single door only. She said we had been given rooms on the same floor for convenience, she as his nurse in case she was needed if he became suddenly ill, and I in case I worked late, for I could return to my room without disturbing anyone.

Erma and the servants all had rooms downstairs at the back of the house, apart from the family dining and living rooms in the front of Valhalla. I turned the corner on the second floor where a long passage led away from the stairs. The passage

had only blank walls; then ahead I saw two doors
facing each other. The door of one was open, the
other closed. That on my right, the open door, dis-
closed a huge man sitting in a deep chair facing
the entrance, stroking a black-and-tan Doberman
pinscher, who obviously sensed my approach and
stared at me with alert, unfriendly eyes.

"You are the Fräulein Mitchell?" the big man
said, getting up, but keeping one hand on the
dog's collar. His voice was deep, but not unfriendly, a voice that suited his size and obvious
strength. The dog growled and crouched, but the
big hand on his collar held him.

"Yes, I am," I said nervously. He had a tough
brown face, with deep lines. His hair was gray, the
hair of a man close to sixty, but still, strangely, he
seemed comparatively youthful. "I was told to
report to Herr Richter's study at seven-thirty."

"You are five minutes early," he said. "It is better to be here on time, Fräulein. But that doesn't
matter this morning. This morning I want to in-
troduce you to my friend Bruno. I am Hans
Freich—Sergeant Hans Freich, some call me.
Bruno and I guard the door opposite at all times.
If one of us is not on duty, the other is. Only those
people Herr Richter wishes to see ever enter that
door. So it is necessary that Bruno recognize you
as a friend, if you are to work in there like the
nurse and the maids. I was warned by phone of
your coming, but Bruno cannot answer phones so
must meet you in person."

The dog stared at me unblinkingly, making no
sound. The man released the collar and put his

hands on either side of the dog's head, talking to it soothingly in a low voice.

"*Friend, Bruno, friend!* This one is new here, but a friend. She will be here every day when the master is in there working, so you must get used to seeing her. He is a highly trained guard dog, Fräulein, and will not trouble you once he has his instructions. And I think he is accepting you already. He has a preference for women, accepting women much easier than men. *Friend, Bruno!* She is a friend. *Good!* Will you come in here quietly, Fräulein? He's prepared to meet you now. Speak to him by name."

I entered nervously. "Bruno! Hello, Bruno. Will you be my friend? Good dog!"

"Put your hand on his head now. No, firmly— they sense fear. Stroke him gently. That's it. I think he likes you, Fräulein. *Friend*, Bruno! This one we must let pass at all times. Good dog. That's enough, Fräulein. Now, go back a few yards along the passage, then walk confidently to Herr Richter's door and ring the bell."

"Should I speak to him when I come back?" I asked Sergeant Freich nervously.

"It is better if you do not. Or even try to stroke him again. Just act as though he and I are not here when you come to work. Once he accepts you, there is no danger, and it is better that he has only one person for whom he feels affection. *Me*." He glanced at a wristwatch. "Go now, and you are right on time. When you are about to ring the bell, do not look at him if you can help it. Some of the maids are too nervous not to look, so he growls at them."

"Thank you, Sergeant." I smiled. "I promise not to look at him."

There was no sound from the dog as I made my approach. I had to fight an impulse to see how Bruno was reacting as I pressed the bell. I heard Sergeant Freich say sternly, *"Sit, Bruno! Friend!"*

Goose pimples ran up and down my back as imagination showed me the Doberman with bared teeth ready to leap upon me from behind. But the door was opening.

Johann Richter stood there, a gaunt frame of a man standing straight with difficulty. "Ah," he said. "Fräulein Mitchell! Right on time. Good! Come in and let us begin."

I looked instinctively for the electronic equipment for opening and locking doors that I'd seen in Paul Richter's laboratory, but there appeared to be none. I had noticed the sturdy bolt outside, and now I saw the double locks on the inside. I wondered about that until I remembered that *Paul* was the electronics expert, and it was his sons that Johann wanted to keep out. Sergeant Hans Freich, Bruno, and the old-fashioned locks were better protection than electronic doors that Paul might tamper with.

"I hope you have fully recovered, Fräulein?"

"I feel fine, Herr Richter, thank you." I smiled.

"Good! Then I will not waste time. The power lines have been repaired, and we have good light this morning. We must make the most of it. As you see, the gale is still blowing outside, and there is intermittent snow. Men will be working outside clearing the drive and the paths, but they have orders to be quiet and not disturb us. Here is where you will work, Fräulein."

The desk was large; there was a modern swivel chair, an electric typewriter, a spare manual one—in fact, everything I needed. It was comfortably warm in the study; a log fire glowed in a huge fireplace. His own big, old-fashioned desk faced down the room toward the open door of a library. I noticed my first piece of electronic equipment then, a security camera aimed toward us.

He noticed my interest, and his lips twisted in a smile. "Closed-circuit television, Fräulein. The equipment is from my own factories in Stuttgart. The camera is for security purposes. The screen is in the opposite corner. See it?"

It was a good picture. It showed me Sergeant Freich's open door, and the man himself sitting in his chair inside the room. Bruno lay beside him, dozing while his master watched. As I stared at him, Sergeant Freich looked up, and it was as though our eyes met, for he smiled.

"Sergeant Freich and Bruno?"

"We can see Freich and he can see us at all times. His TV screen is above his door."

"You seem to have very tight security here, Herr Richter." I smiled.

"I wish it were not necessary, Fräulein," he said, frowning. "But unfortunately, I know that it is. And if you are to work with me, you too must be subject to it. Nothing that you read or are told in here must ever be repeated outside this room."

True.
Unexpected taste

5 MGS. TAR, 0.4 MGS. NICOTINE

© Lorillard, U.S.A., 1978

5 MG TAR

Warning: The Surgeon General Has Determined That Cigarette Smoking Is Dangerous to Your Health.

Regular and Menthol: 5 mg. "tar", 0.4 mg. nicotine av. per cigarette, FTC Report Aug. 1977.

Newport

©Lorillard, U.S.A., 1977

Newport

MENTHOL KINGS

Alive with pleasure!

17 mg. "tar", 1.2 mg.
nicotine av. per cigarette,
FTC Report Aug. 1977.

Warning: The Surgeon General Has Determined
That Cigarette Smoking Is Dangerous to Your Health.

Faded blue eyes were studying me intently. His grim smile showed fleetingly again. "You do not seem surprised, Fräulein? So they have already been at you, prying, bullying, trying to make you promise to act the spy for them against their own father. It would be Paul, of course, principally Paul, but Herman too in a lesser degree. Erma thinks as they do, but doesn't have the same incentives or the same effrontery."

When I did not answer, he nodded. "You are a good choice, I think, Fräulein! You have the wisdom of silence, I see. May I ask what you told . . . this person who is pestering you for information?"

"I said an employer should be able to rely on the loyalty of his secretary, Herr Richter. If whatever I type or translate you ask me to keep confidential, I will do that. There is no way I would disclose it to anyone else, including your sons."

He nodded, obviously pleased. "Good! But I intend to make it easier for you than the moral obligation of a secretary toward her employer, Fräulein. I have a paper for you to read and sign. Afterward, if you are asked questions, you can say you cannot answer because of the agreement. Let them blame me, not you." He walked over to his desk and sat down. "Hans," he said conversationally, "come in here. I have need for a witness to the Fräulein's signature on a paper."

"Coming, Herr Richter," Hans Freich's deep voice said from the television. I glanced up instinctively, and he was getting up. The dog sprang to his feet at once and looked up at him alertly. "Watch, Bruno!" he said sternly. "Watch!"

"Draw up a chair, Fräulein, and read this. It is a simple agreement that I am sure you will easily understand. Yet is is legally binding, I assure you."

It was short and simple, I saw, reading as Sergeant Freich unlocked the outer door and came in to stand silently waiting. Then I came to the penalty clause and read it, and returned to read it again. I did some rapid mental arithmetic.

"The amount in the penalty clause is exactly what my total salary will be for six months. You said the memoirs would take six months to complete. This would mean I would receive nothing."

He smiled. "Only if you passed on the information, Fräulein," he reminded me gently. "Which I am sure you will not do. I have complete faith in your discretion and loyalty. I mean in fact to add a handsome bonus to the sum I mentioned as salary in my letter, once the memoirs are safely at the publisher's office. In the meantime, Fräulein, sign this paper, and you have an excellent argument to use against the pressures my sons and perhaps even my niece Erma will be bringing to bear upon you."

I signed, and Sergeant Freich scrawled a bold signature beneath mine, then departed. Johann put the agreement in a wall safe near his desk and momentarily, as he turned to stare at me, I saw a different, a much more unpleasant Johann Richter.

"It is possible that my sons might outbid me, of

course," he said, his faded blue eyes cold as ice suddenly. "That they may offer you more than the salary and a bonus of a thousand dollars that I intend to give you if you keep our bargain. . . ."

"I don't take bribes!" I protested angrily.

"Hear me out," he said sternly. "And be warned, Fräulein. If you *should* be so foolish as to forget the agreement and forgo your fee, there are other ways by which you can be stopped from betraying me. Remember that. There are other, more severe penalties that I have arranged to have imposed upon you. The penalties are such that, if you were ever tempted to betray me, I am certain you would deeply regret your treachery while you lived."

"You're threatening me?" I stared at him unbelievingly.

He sat down heavily in the chair behind his desk.

"Circumstances force me to threaten you, Fräulein," he said wearily. "I have said what I have to say. Let us go to work and not speak of it again."

"But . . ." I wanted to get up and go, to leave Valhalla forever. Then I remembered again that I had no money. "Very well," I said. "I am ready, Herr Richter."

"Then here is the first chapter," he said, unlocking a drawer in his desk and taking out a manila folder. He smiled in relief, I noticed, as he brought it to my desk. "I want you to read this and ask any questions you need to know to convert my poor attempt at literature into the finished manuscript. You will find some passages still in German, which you will translate. Can you do this?"

I nodded. "I was doing work like this in California, as I told you."

"Good!" he said. "Then go to work." He showed me a button on the desk before me. "Remember that whatever we say in here, Hans hears on the set in his room, as we hear in here whatever he says. Hans and I have been together for a long time, Fräulein. We are friends. Therefore, I do not want Hans involved by knowing any of the details of our work. He could be put under much more severe pressures than you to disclose them. Therefore, when you have a question to ask me, or a paragraph you need to read to me, first press your button like this."

I heard the faint click as he pressed, and on the television set Sergeant Freich looked up quickly and nodded.

"You see. The sound of our voices has stopped in Hans's set. Your button switched off all sound. Make sure you use it, Fräulein."

"Very well, Herr Richter."

I opened the folder, settled down, and began to read.

★ 6 ★

I quickly became interested in Johann Richter's memoirs. He wrote fluently and forcefully in German, but had trouble translating his best thoughts into English. Whole paragraphs, sometimes whole pages, were still in German, which I must translate, type, and present for his inspection while we discussed nuances of meaning in trying to find the English words that best described what he wanted to say. Only then, when we had decided on the best word, the best phrase, could I type and incorporate the passage into the section of finished manuscript.

All this took time. Time that I knew Johann Richter could not afford. He still had quite a large section of the book to write. While I read, translated, corrected, and typed, he was trying to write original literature from the contents of diaries, worn notebooks, and his memory. I couldn't help noticing the effort it cost him to regain his concentration each time I had to interrupt him.

In this first chapter that he had given me, Johann was a poor, demobilized conscript who had fought in World War One but could not find a job after the armistice. It was a human document of the political and economic bankruptcy of a nation, as seen through the eyes of a young man trying to climb out of the depths of degradation and poverty toward wealth and power.

He must certainly have been a determined and ambitious young man. It was this driving lust for wealth and power which best described the character of the young Johann Richter. And then I realized something else. Although he probably did not know it, in describing his own character, Johann was describing his son Paul.

The wind and the snowfall began to abate as the week, my first at Valhalla, passed. On Wednesday we had a visitor.

I was puzzling over the exact meaning of a word when I heard Sergeant Freich's voice boom from the television set. The set had been silent ever since Elsa had left after tidying up Herr Richter's private rooms early in the morning, so I looked up startled. A young man, carrying what looked like a wooden traveling bag smeared with paint in one hand, and a dilapidated canvas carryall in the other, stood frozen in the opposite doorway, watching Sergeant Freich holding back with difficulty a ferocious Bruno intent upon devouring the intruder.

"Down, Bruno! Down!" Sergeant Freich was shouting. "Friend, Bruno! Friend!"

I watched the angry dog quieten slowly and lie down. Sergeant Freich said grimly, "It is well not to appear suddenly *here*, mein Herr! And you are twenty-three minutes late! With the weather as it is, we had decided you were not coming, so your sudden appearance surprised us. You are lucky I caught Bruno before he attacked you!"

"I'm glad you did!" Rick Byron said with feeling. "Thanks!"

Sergeant Freich began to release the dog carefully, and I looked at Johann Richter. His head was still bent over the page he was writing, his lips moving as they formed silent words. He was too engrossed to notice when I began hurried repairs to my makeup. He had quite forgotten poor Rick was coming, I decided.

I put my makeup away as Rick crossed warily to the door and rang the bell. "It's the artist from Fifeness village, Herr Richter," I said. "His name is Byron, Rick Byron. You commissioned him to paint your portrait for the book."

He finished typing the sentence he was working on before he looked up. "Artist? Oh, yes, of course!" He studied the visitor on the TV screen at the end of the study. "You know him?"

"We met in the village the night I came here."

"I'd forgotten. He was taking you to the village boardinghouse when Paul came along, wasn't he? I didn't expect him to come to Valhalla in this weather, but since he is here, let him in."

Rick probably needed the money, I thought, getting up quickly to open the door. He grinned at me. "Hi!" he said in English. "You look great on television. You're in the wrong occupation."

I smiled. "I thought all you saw out there was Bruno!"

"Not after I recognized you on the sceen behind him," he said. "Do I come in?"

"Herein!" I stood aside for him. "Do you speak German?"

"I learned German at high school," he said proudly in that language, "and continued in college."

I winced. His accent was atrocious. "Herr Richter likes everyone here to speak German at all times." I gave him a warning glance. "If you get into difficulties, ask me. I'll try to help."

"Thanks," he said. "I'll take you up on that. Herr Richter and I don't seem to speak quite the same German. Sometimes he has difficulty understanding me. Maybe it's because he comes from one of the provinces."

"Maybe it's because you come from America," I said, shutting the door.

"Smart aleck!" he muttered.

I went back to my desk and bent my head over my work again. Rick went through into one of the rooms in Herr Richter's private suite and began to set up his easel, drawing materials, and paints. Herr Richter finally went in to where he waited patiently, and the sitting began.

Working, I forgot them both until they came out again, and by then it was time for lunch. I walked downstairs with Rick and Herr Richter. Herr Richter, I noticed, seemed to like Rick. He even joked about his pronunciation and corrected him. Rick tried to follow what he suggested, but was comically hopeless.

Johann turned into the living room, and I noticed Adrienne in there with Herman and Paul as I walked past with Rick Byron. They did not notice us, for which I was grateful.

"Did you get much done this morning?" I asked.

"I made a start," Rick said, smiling at me. He had the most guileless gray eyes I'd ever seen in a man, I noticed. I had decided I liked him at our first meeting in Fifeness. This morning seemed to have strengthened my impression.

"When . . . are you coming back?" I asked. I had almost said: "When will I see you again?"

"He suggested I come here each day until the portrait is finished. Except Sundays, which he tells me are his days of rest. The portrait will take some time. I like to study my subject, and I paint only from sketches in oils. He wants it finished in approximately sixteen weeks, he said. He seems to be working to a time limit. What is it writers call that?"

"A deadline."

"That's it! I can have it completed for his deadline. Only . . ."

"Only what, Rick?" His first name had seemed to slip out. Because that was the way I had been thinking of him, I supposed. But he did not seem to notice.

"Herr Richter seems to me to be a sick man," he said slowly. "It's only a few days since I saw him, but I noticed a change in him. I'm wondering if he's working too hard for his strength." He hesitated. "He's a generous man, and I want to give him his money's worth. A man whose weight, color, and facial characteristics are changing rapidly through illness is difficult to paint. I mean, how to paint him? As I see him now? Or as he may be three months from now?"

"He is a sick man."

We had come to the door, and I opened it for him.

He looked at me seriously. "Can you tell me what's the matter with him?"

I shook my head. "He would have to do that, Rick."

He frowned. "I see. Then, as I suspected, it must be bad. Okay, I won't ask you that again. I've heard rumors in the village, of course. . . . Do you think he's working too hard for his strength in his present state of heath?"

"Everyone here thinks so. But he's determined to finish the book, no matter what happens."

"I would think his relatives would stop him, slow him down."

"They would if they could." But not for the reason Rick had in mind.

"He's a man of great determination, then?" he probed.

"I would say so."

"Then that's the way I'll paint him," he said. "A little younger than he is today. A little, but not too much, healthier." He put his head out the door and shivered. "Brrr! Why did I ever leave Florida?"

"Or I California?" I said.

"See you tomorrow. By the way, they have a village dance in Fifeness every Saturday night. Everyone mixes, and they almost, but not quite, forget you're a foreigner and not really from good old Maine. They've always got something going, like someone puts on a clambake, or roasts chestnuts, or if it's summer, organizes a hayride. It might do you good to get away from this place for a night, and there is always a spare bed for everyone at the widow's on Saturday nights. Will you think about it? Plenty of time for you to decide. Okay?"

"Okay," I said. "I'll think about it."

The gardeners had been clearing the snow from the drive. They had banked it high on either side, but they seemed to be fighting a losing battle, for Rick was sinking almost to his boot tops as he climbed into a battered and aging Chevy with chains around its wheels.

Seeing my interest, he paused with the door open before sliding inside the car out of the cold wind. "Mostly I walk!" he informed me, grinning. "But not in weather like this. I borrowed it from one of the fishermen. See you!" The car door banged.

"Tomorrow!" I said, and closed the door of Valhalla hurriedly against the cold. The car started, and he drove away as I walked back toward the living room. I thought it appropriate that he didn't own a car. It fit in with the bohemian image Paul had given him. But then, neither had many students I'd known in California. They were not dropouts. Some of their parents had plenty of money. Probably even more than the Richter family. You never could tell about things like that.

I wished he hadn't made the little village dance sound so inviting, though. I felt I wouldn't mind going. Especially since Johann never worked on Sundays.

Paul Richter glared at me suspiciously as I walked into the living room. I smiled at him sweetly and crossed to the fire to thaw out. Adrienne and Herman, talking quietly where they sat together farther away from the heat of the blazing log fire, barely noticed my entry, but Paul drew up a chair beside mine.

"That was the artist you were farewelling?"

"Yes."

"He started painting the portrait?"

I glanced at the chair beyond him, where his father, leaning back, was beginning to doze. Lines of utter fatigue showed on his face, made ruddy by the warmth.

"Yes."

Paul lowered his voice. "I hope you haven't forgotten the warning I gave you in the village. And that you will heed it, Fräulein."

"I like to make up my own mind about things like that, Herr Richter," I said coldly. "As I told you then."

"You do not understand the situation, Lorna!" he said resentfully.

"Warning? What warning did you give her, Paul?" He had not opened his eyes, but Johann Richter had asked the question.

Paul glanced at him sourly. "I warned her

against the man, Father," Paul said bitterly. "And why not? He's just another vagrant. What the Americans call a hippie. He has little talent. I have seen his daubs displayed in the village, and I know."

"So now you have become a judge of the quality of art, eh, Paul?" Johann's eyes remained wearily closed, I saw. His expression was disinterested.

"You will regret your choice, Father, you will see," Paul said arrogantly. "Such worthless people are a source of trouble, as you will discover. If I could have advised you, he would not be here. But apparently you prefer to make your plans in secret where they concern your writing. You will not listen to advice, even from your sons. You should take Herman and me into your confidence about this thing. The employment of the artist is a mistake, and it is not your first."

"What makes you think you have the right to pry into my affairs, Paul?" his father asked coldly.

"I am your son. So is Herman," Paul said, growing angry. "If it comes to that, what makes you think you have the right to advertise our private lives by writing a book about us?"

"I am not concerned with your private life, Paul," Johann said quietly. "I write of my own, and that is no concern of yours. While I am the head of this house I have the right to do that. And I will. Do I ask you what you do behind the locked doors of your laboratory? Do I demand to know the formulae of your experiments? Would you give them to me if I did?"

Paul Richter shook his head angrily and got up.

He stalked out of the room without answering. Johann leaned back in his chair and let him go.

"Paul didn't mean to offend you, Father," Herman said placatively from where he sat with Adrienne. "He thinks, and so do I, that you should discuss the memoirs with us. Perhaps even let us help you compile them. There must be dates, incidents in the past that seem vague to you now. That you might misinterpret in your present state of health. You work too hard. We could save you that. We could research what you have forgotten. Our minds are younger and more alert than yours. We may be able to describe more accurately those events that left vivid impressions. We want to help you, Father. Both of us."

"I have no doubt of that," Johann said cuttingly. The maid had appeared, but sensing the chilly atmosphere, was hovering uncertainly in the doorway. Johann noticed her and heaved himself painfully to his feet. "Lunch is ready. Shall we go in? We must lunch without Paul today it seems."

We rose obediently to follow him into the dining room.

As we walked inside, Adrienne muttered indignantly, "You were the cause of that, Lorna! You got poor Paul and Herman into trouble. Couldn't you have let what Paul said pass, without arguing about it?"

I was about to protest angrily, but remembered there didn't seem to be anything wrong with Johann's hearing. He had sharp ears for anything people didn't want him to hear. So I said nothing. Adrienne, made more angry by my lack of response, put her nose in the air, and her brown eyes flashed. Knowing Adrienne, I decided she probably wouldn't speak to me again today.

She didn't speak to me again all week, except to be coldly polite when for some reason, as when she came to the study to give Johann his pills, she found it unavoidable. I think that prompted me to agree to go to the dance in Fifeness with Rick when he asked the next day. At least that was one of the reasons. Rick was the other.

Johann raised no objection, when, deciding I should let him know, I asked him what he thought about it. We seemed to be getting along well, Herr Johann Richter and I. I had already made several suggestions to make our work smoother and faster, which he accepted gratefully. Now he was working uninterruptedly with the creative writing and I on typing and translating. We went into conference on my choice of English words for only one session at the end of each day. And those sessions were becoming shorter as his confidence grew in my ability to express in English translation exactly what he meant. I rarely had to retype a page of the finished manuscript. Under the old system I had to type every page twice.

On Thursday night he decided to work late, and I with him, and again on Friday night. Working late with Johann meant working until he practically collapsed at his desk, and the night was almost over. I would stagger back to my room and fall on the bed. The maid had to shake me awake each morning, because no matter how late he worked at night, Johann would be in the study waiting for me to appear at seven-thirty in the morning.

He could be considerate, though, I discovered on Saturday afternoon when he asked abruptly, "How do you propose to get to the village tonight? Does he have an automobile?"

I smiled. "He borrows one."

"You could have had my car and the chauffeur. The weather has improved enough to use the limousine. But no matter. What do they do at these occasions?"

"Rick . . . Herr Byron said tonight is a square dance."

"Square dance?" He stared at me over his glasses uncomprehendingly.

"It's an informal dance where the people wear working clothes. The type of music is fairly old by American standards. There is a revival of that sort of thing at the moment. For dances they have a caller who chants the next move. They have a heavy supper, and they dance for most of the night."

"I see! They dress, eat, drink, and behave like peasants!"

"Hold on, Herr Richter," I began to protest, remembering how his son Paul had said: "The people here are all ignorant, narrow-minded peasants!"

He chuckled though, with a happy sound that stopped me abruptly before he said, "Good! In Germany we did such things before the war. There was a revival of them in the thirties, as you say you have here now. We danced polkas and folk dances, and there was also jazz. Paul was just a little boy. To such a place I used to take Gisela, my wife, as you will read very soon in my memoirs. We had no money, and little food; we were very poor. We had to make our own fun, or have none—so we did. Dancing was cheap, so we danced. Some young men and women played musical instruments. We would use someone's home to dance in, or if we had a few marks, we might hire some derelict public hall. They were good days, Fräulein. They were the days to remember."

"And you have not forgotten?"

"Never!" he said. "I even remember how long my Gisela used to take dressing up for our dances, Fräulein. You, too, I am sure, will want to look your best tonight. So off with you now."

"But . . ."

"I too will stop. I will go to bed early tonight, and tomorrow, Sunday, is my day of rest. But remember, I will work you the harder next week for it!"

I laughed, delighted. I would tell Adrienne this, I decided—when she got over her bad temper, as she must soon. We never could be angry with each other for very long. But I remembered how she had changed. Or perhaps how the Richters had changed her.

Rick called for me in a truck that smelled of fish. The weather had been too bad for the Fifeness fishermen to put to sea for some time, so the smell of fish was strong, to say the least of it, despite the freezing weather. I wore jeans, and so did Rick. But the jeans didn't mean that I didn't have to take time with my shower, my makeup, and my hair. Rick said he thought I looked great.

I was shy at first when he walked me into a crowded hall packed with strange people of all ages, sitting on hard benches around the walls and all dressed much as we were. There were only a few dresses, and those seemed to me to suffer in comparison to jeans. But everyone was friendly and smiling, like folk out to enjoy a night's entertainment.

I was new to square dancing, so Rick had to show me what to do at first. Then I began to catch on, and had a terrific time. I was sorry when the caller announced that supper was ready and would we all file past the kitchen with our plates before the roast pork and clam chowder got cold and spoiled. He had forgotten to mention the onion-and-peanut sauce the widow Clout had made from her own recipe, or her apple pie with whipped cream.

I was introduced to the widow Clout—nobody ever seemed to call her anything else but that. She was a plump and smiling woman whom everyone seemed to like. I learned she had been the Valhalla housekeeper before the Richters came to Fifeness. When I admired her delicious roast pork and clam chowder, she said that was nothing. I should come to a Saturday-night dance in the summer, when Margaret Parsons, the fisherman's wife, steamed fresh lobsters and whole clams over hot rocks and seaweed and served them piping hot with melted butter. I told her with my mouth watering that I could hardly wait.

It was a happy night, with everyone having fun. Some of the men kept disappearing, and Rick said there was a keg of mead outside that one of the guys who was an apiarist had brought in from his bee farm.

Mead! It reminded me of Sir Walter Scott novels.

I was surprised when someone said it was two A.M. and some of the families were dairy farmers who had cows to milk in the early morning. There was snow everywhere outside when we began to straggle from the hall, but it had stopped snowing and even the wind had dropped to an almost gentle breeze. The air was clean and invigoratingly cold. I could even see some stars through a break in the clouds. The widow Clout had driven home with her dishes from the supper. I walked home slowly to the widow's house with Rick, past the corner where we had sheltered from the storm and Paul Richter had picked me up so rudely.

The widow's house was about what I expected after meeting her. As crisp and clean as the woman herself, and as welcoming. In my room the sheets had that freshly laundered smell, with a difference that I decided could only be dried lavender. The blankets were soft and warm as a caress, and there was even a patchwork quilt on the bed.

I tried the widow's coffee that Rick had boasted about, and we sat in the warm and frilly guest lounge drinking it with the other people who were staying overnight.

One by one the others went to bed, but we talked on in low voices, learning things about each other. When he walked to the door of my room with me, it seemed the most natural thing in the world that we should kiss good night. And that, I decided as I went to bed, made the night just about one of the best I remembered. My head no sooner touched the pillow than I fell asleep.

It was late afternoon before we left the village and Rick drove me home to Valhalla, this time in the widow's own car, a VW bug that was her pride and joy. He said he borrowed it only on special occasions.

"If anything happened to it"—he smiled—"it would be like losing a child to her. She has no family of her own. Maybe that's why she's so kind to us strays."

I laughed and told him I'd met people like that in Europe as an *au pair* girl. "Why don't you get a car of your own?" I asked. "Or is that asking a silly question? Artists never have much money, do they?"

"What about Pablo Picasso?" he asked me indignantly. "Will you ride with me Sundays if I do buy one?"

"I'll think about it," I said. "But don't buy one just for me. You might need the money for something else." Artists had to eat too, after all.

At least he drove carefully on the cliff road. Today that seemed easy enough in daylight. Like most of the other cars in Fifeness in winter, the widow's car had chains on its wheels. The seas beating at the foot of the cliff were still high, but vehicles had passed along the road between the village and the house, so there were tracks in the snow that we could follow safely enough, even if the ground beneath the snow was frozen and slippery.

"I like to paint in weather like this when the light is right," he said as we cleared the Devil's Bend and entered safer road. "I'd be out catching the sea in this mood on Monday if I could. But I want to finish the sketch in oils I'm working on."

"Will you start on the full portrait next week, then?" I asked.

"That depends on whether I'm satisfied with the sketch. Probably not. I usually need to make at least three sketches in oils before I'm satisfied with the subject's expression."

I frowned. "You sound as though you've painted other portraits."

"One or two," he admitted, glancing at me mischievously. "But we're almost there, so we don't have time for me to tell you about my artistic career. I've had my moments of victory." He changed the subject as we reached the gates of Valhalla. "I'll tell you about them someday. When can I see you again, Lorna? Soon?"

"Monday, I'd say." I smiled. "If Bruno lets you in."

"Sergeant Freich is on my side."

"And just as well!"

"I didn't mean when will I see you *at work*, I meant like this." He shook his head. "If I buy a car, the way I see it, I'm entitled to one attractive passenger. Female. You. Okay?"

"It would have to be Sunday."

"For both of us," he reminded me.

I glanced up at the unfriendly bulk of stone mansion ahead and wished I was staying in Fifeness village at the widow Clout's. But I didn't tell Rick that. Lights were coming on in Valhalla. There were lights in the ground-floor living room. Adrienne and Herman must be in there sipping drinks before the fire, I decided. And maybe Paul too, though he was unpredictable.

Rick stopped the Volkswagen with a flourish at the foot of the main-entrance steps. "Far as we go," he said. "What about next Sunday?"

"We have all week to discuss that, Rick," I said. "Thanks for the wonderful weekend."

I hadn't consciously intended to kiss him, but I did. I withdrew from him with difficulty, a little scared by his response.

"I'll see you tomorrow—at work," I murmured.

He nodded, and I went up the steps and rang the bell, hearing him turn the car back toward the gates. It gave a faint toot, and I waved. The door was opening as I pressed the bell. I smiled, expecting Elsa's round, pleasant face. I froze momentarily. Paul Richter was staring at me angrily, his face pale and his blue eyes glittering.

"You kissed that shiftless bum!" he hissed at me jealously. "You stay out with him all night! You kiss him when he leaves you!"

He had no right to be jealous of me. I said

coldly, "Were you peeping, Herr Richter? I didn't see *you* until you opened the door."

"I warned you against these people. I forbade you to fraternize with them!"

I forced myself to smile. "You don't have the right to forbid me doing anything, Herr Richter," I said. "To fraternize, as you put it, or anything else. Now, do you mind—it's cold out here."

I brushed past him and stepped into the passage. Momentarily I expected him to grab me again as he had in his laboratory. I felt the surge of strength against me as I passed him, but if he was so inclined, he changed his mind.

"You are the only attractive girl I've met in this country, Lorna," he said in a low, almost pleading voice. "I could grow to like you, don't you realize that? Are you a fool? I could even marry a girl like you. . . ."

I walked on as though I hadn't heard. I reached the stairs and turned toward my room. In the living room I heard Adrienne's laughter and Herman's voice telling her something amusing. At the landing I glanced back unobstrusively.

Paul Richter still stood at the open door staring up at me. In my room I remembered the jealous hatred I had seen in his eyes as he accused me.

★ 7 ★

The ravages of the brain tumor were becoming more apparent in Johann Richter's bloodless face. There were times when I doubted that he would live to finish his memoirs. Occasionally I would see him falter at his desk, and it was as though only his indomitable will kept him working. In his ashen, pain-lined face, sometimes only the faded blue eyes seemed alive.

The progress of the disease was as apparent to his family, for their pressure upon him and upon me seemed to ease. At times during a meal when he barely toyed with his food, I could detect a sly, triumphant gleam in the eyes of his sons when they looked at him.

Only his niece Erma, womanlike, looked at him with sympathy.

Adrienne thawed that weekend. She came into my bedroom on Sunday night and kissed me and said she was sorry. As always when we had some foolish argument, she wept a little. I never have been able to resist her tears, and I was unable to now. Afterward I had to tell her all about my weekend, and she listened—a little enviously I

116

thought. She never had been a girl to be content in one place. Or in the company of one man, either, if it came to that.

We worked harder in Johann Richter's suite than I would have thought possible. I was so weary at night that once I sank into bed, I rarely moved before morning. But the results of our hard work were becoming increasingly apparent. The finished manuscript was growing steadily, much more quickly than he had hoped for.

"It is because of your idea to study the translation in its completed form," he told me seriously late one night when, with the great house sleeping, we finished the day's editing. "Your work now is completed in not much more than half the time. It is I who am the handicap." I discovered him studying me almost with affection. "If that fertile young brain of yours could only discover some way to prod an old man into working faster . . ."

I smiled and shook my head. "Nobody can work beyond his strength, Herr Richter. Do that, and you will produce less, not more. The answer can't be there."

"Where is it, then, Fräulein?" he asked, puzzling.

"I would say in using what strength you have to the best advantage. I have been thinking about that. Do you have confidence in my translation of your work?"

"Much more than I ever thought possible, Fräulein," he said. "Only occasionally now is there something that does not seem quite what I want to say. And even there, I have to admit that my knowledge of English is not as good as yours. Therefore my doubt may be, and sometimes is, wrong. Which we adjust between us."

I smiled. "Exactly, Herr Richter. Some study and revision of words we have to expect. Now, when could you find time to study my typed pages without that interfering with your creative writing?"

He shook his head, frowning. "In bed perhaps, or on Sundays?"

"But then you would not be resting, and you must have your rest."

"The only time I do not work is when I sit for your friend Herr Byron, the artist. I have thought of abandoning the idea of a portrait for the book, but it is something the publishers demand. They seem to think this is necessary."

"But they do not say how the portrait should be painted? Whether you, the subject, should be standing, or seated before your typewriter, whether your hands should be folded one upon the other or holding a book, or what-have-you?"

"They left that to the artist. Naturally."

"Why not have you seated and studying a manuscript? Herr Byron told me he likes to make three sketches in oils before he commences the portrait. Why not ask him about this when he comes tomorrow to start the second sketch?"

"And if I worked then on the typed pages, queried any word I felt I had to, and made a note of it . . . ?" He looked at me. "You could then take it from there, Fräulein? This would almost eliminate the hour we spend together checking each night. It would save me an hour each day."

"I think it could."

"Brilliant!" he said, trying to smile, but too weary. "What else do you have, Fräulein?"

"I've been thinking about the way you work, Herr Richter." I hesitated. "I mean no offense, but you write fluently and in my opinion brilliantly in German. You rarely need to alter a word of it. I estimate that it takes you twice as long each day for the English translation as it does for the original pages, *the original creative writing typed in German.* Would you agree?"

He frowned. "But of course, that is obvious . . ." He broke off. "You mean if you did the whole translation . . . ?"

"How long would it take you to finish the memoirs if you wrote only in German, Herr Richter?"

He was staring at me. "I could finish it in six weeks, Fräulein. Not six *months,* as I first planned!"

"And with much less work, conserving your strength?"

"Why, yes!"

"And if we took even part of the time you would save and put that into our checking, you would still be way ahead on your schedule, wouldn't you, Herr Richter?"

"Yes!"

"So why don't we try it?"

"Yes!" he said. "Yes, Fräulein! Why, if I could only save . . ." He broke off. "But you? What about you, Fräulein? Do you realize how much work this would give you?"

"So I would work late nights and on Sundays if I had to. I am younger and in better health than you are. And I have worked hard before. I promise not to complain. After all, what is there to do here, except go to the Saturday-night dance in the village?"

He was staring at me, shaking his head. "You would do this for me, Fräulein? Why?"

I shrugged. "I think I can understand how much it means to you to see your book in print. To discover what people think about it, and read in newspapers what the critics have to say. Would you drive yourself to the limit of your strength in your state of health if these things were not vitally important to you?"

"This is true," he said simply. "The memoirs mean more to me than life. The truth means more to me than life. And this, it seems to me, is the only way left by which it can ever be told."

"Then this is what we must do, Herr Richter," I said.

"There is one other thing, Fräulein," he said slowly. "When you agreed to come here to work with me, you gave me the impression in your letter of application that you had very little money, that you needed this work. And that of course means that you needed the money you would earn?"

"Yes."

"Yet you are prepared to do the same work in half the time, which in terms of our agreement means that you will lose half of what you could have earned."

I smiled. "Sometimes I do what some people would consider foolish things, Herr Richter. But only when doing them brings me satisfaction. Good night, Herr Richter."

"I promise you, if you help me do this, Fräulein, you will not lose by it or regret what you do," he said. He closed the door behind me, and I sighed wearily. The door directly opposite, as always, stood wide open. The only sound within was Sergeant Freich's heavy breathing as he slept while Bruno stood guard.

The dog watched me intently from where it sat in the doorway without sound or movement. A perfect black-and-tan statue rather than a living, breathing dog. Grown used to seeing it there now, I turned toward the stairs and my own suite. The dog watched me go, and I noticed as I reached the turn in the passage that from where it sat it could watch the whole length of the passage on either side.

The work became harder. I saw less of Adrienne and Herman. But I saw Paul often, for he seemed to go out of his way to be near me. I avoided him when I could. When we met, he was coldly polite, but I could see hatred in his bleak blue eyes.

I saw Rick every day except Sundays though, and no matter how hard I worked, seeing Rick's affectionate smile seemed to make it all worthwhile. We went again to the dance in Fifeness, but I did not stay overnight at the widow's house.

I had Rick drive me home to the great stone house, for now I had to work Sundays while Johann rested. Under the new system I had suggested, I found I could barely keep up, even working seven days a week.

Paul did not greet me jealously at the door, but I saw his shadow on the draperies of his room, watching as we said good night. I kissed Rick more deeply and lingeringly because of that. Well, partly anyway.

I worked late on Sunday night, trying to catch up. I worked until I began to realize through the fog of weariness that my work was suffering.

When I wakened reluctantly to a new week of work on Monday morning, I learned from the maid that Johann was ill and Adrienne had had to call the doctor to him late Sunday night. After examining him, Dr. Brewster had ordered him to stay in bed all day Monday. The maid said she thought she should call me because she knew how hard I had been working lately in order to keep up with Herr Richter and that I might be able to use today to get ahead.

I thanked Elsa for the thought. I wished I *could* get ahead. Johann had been writing so fast lately that I seemed getting farther and farther behind. Still, if I worked today, gained a day's work, I could catch up somewhat.

When the girl had left me, I walked over to draw the window draperies and peer out, as I usually did, to see what kind of day it was. Weak sunlight dazzled my overworked eyes. There was mist clinging to the sea, and most of the sky was filled with heavy cloud. But the sun was shining on part of a gray sea and on this eastern side of Valhalla. From my window I could see part of the cliff road near the sidetrack to the chauffeur's house. About to draw the draperies again and dress for work, I froze, staring.

A pickup truck was moving slowly toward the Connell house from the cliff road. I knew that truck and its stale-fish smell. It was the fisherman's truck Rick sometimes borrowed. Staring intently, I decided that it was Rick's gear I could see in the back of the truck. The easel that folded into a hinged wooden box, the paint-smeared bag, the yellow windbreaker he wore in bad weather.

Fear touched me suddenly. The truck was lurching, turning out of the side road and beginning to climb the slope that formed the side of the little valley that more distantly became the cliff-top above the Devil's Bend. What on earth was Rick doing? I felt sick watching, fearing he would turn the truck over and roll back down to the road to the Connell place.

But the truck continued steadily climbing, lurching less now as it climbed diagonally across the slope. There must be another track there, I realized. And one quite clearly marked, for there was snow carpeting the whole slope, quite unaffected by this morning's weak sunlight.

I let the bath the maid had run for me grow cold, watching, while the truck climbed to the top of the slope and vanished over the crest. I decided Johann must have had someone, perhaps Dr. Brewster, contact Rick at the widow's to let him know about today being a day of rest. I thought ruefully that maybe Johann Richter was getting to know Rick and me too well! With Rick not coming to Valhalla today, what was there for poor little me to do but work? And Rick, the traitor, was only too eager to take full advantage of Johann's unexpected rest day and the break in the atrocious weather we had been having to paint those wild seas battering the cliff below the Devil's Bend.

Adrienne slept late and did not come down for breakfast. I expected to have to eat alone with Paul, and nervously anticipating his appearance, hurried the light breakfast I chose, with one eye on the door, and escaped before he arrived.

In the opposite doorway Sergeant Freich sat stolidly upon his chair while Bruno roamed casually about the small apartment behind him, obviously enjoying his off-duty period. Occasionally through our television sets we exchanged a few words, for my heart was not in my work alone in the study this morning. I kept thinking about Rick perched on the high cliff above the Devil's Bend capturing on canvas the wild scene below.

I never had seen Rick at work, for in here he painted in another room, to which I had no access. I had seen the first completed sketch in oils. When he showed it to me, I thought it terrific. Now I truly wanted to see him at work, and I might never have a better chance than today.

Perhaps I was seeking an excuse to stop work. But by lunchtime I had just about decided to put on warm clothes and walk over there to take a look. It was not all that far from Valhalla, I knew. I'd run almost the whole of the distance that first night. Walking there, except for the climb to the top of the cliff, would not be any problem.

By lunchtime I had completely convinced myself that I had had enough of the tensions of Valhalla. Bruno had taken over the watch across the passage, and Sergeant Freich was someplace inside having the lunch that one of the maids had already brought up for him. I was early for lunch. Adrienne and Herman came down when I was almost finished, and I made my escape as quickly as I could. Paul, Adrienne remarked, had gone off to the village in one of the jeeps and would probably lunch there, which suited me fine.

It was quite plesant outside. I appreciated the crisp, clean air as I walked out the gates and started toward the Devil's Bend. Only then I heard the jeep coming behind me, and thought: Oh God! Paul! He must have changed his mind about staying in town. My mind raced, seeking an excuse for my walk. One thing was certain, I wasn't going to get into the jeep with Paul Richter.

I walked off the road into deeper snow, stubbornly refusing to look behind me as the sound of the jeep's motor grew louder, then slowed beside me.

"Guten Tag, Fräulein Mitchell," a man's voice said pleasantly. "Are you by any chance going into the village?"

I let my breath sigh out in relief as I recognized Sergeant Freich's voice, not Paul Richter's. I smiled. "I was just walking, Sergeant. Do me good. I mean to work again later and perhaps tonight."

The jeep kept pace with me, and he was smiling cheerfully. "I thought you might have been on your way to join your friend Herr Byron. I noticed him at work with his brushes and paints on the hill behind the Devil's Bend. I thought I'd stop to offer you a ride up the hill, as the climb is so steep. But no matter. . . ."

"Rick's still up there painting?" I asked quickly. "I noticed him there earlier."

"Yes, Fräulein. I saw him through the window of my bedroom with the binoculars, setting up his easel and looking as though he intends to stay up there and paint all day. It is my job to see things like that, as you know. Nothing that moves anywhere near Valhalla escapes me. But of course, if visiting Herr Byron was not your intention . . ."

"I wasn't going anywhere in particular. But if, as you say, Herr Byron is still there . . . You don't think I would be intruding?"

"I would say certainly not, Fräulein." He smiled, still holding the jeep to my walking pace.

"It would be taking you out of your way if you're going to the village. You would have to drive all the way back to the sidetrack. And I know how difficult it is for you to get away from the house. So . . ."

He smiled. "It would be no inconvenience, Fräulein," he said heartily. "I know every high place around Valhalla, just as I know every track that leads to these places. So you see, if I drive you up there, I know another way down that will bring me back onto the cliff road halfway to the village."

"Well, if you're sure it's no bother."

He chuckled and stopped the jeep at once, opening the door and unfolding a rug for me to put around me. "It is good for two young people who like each other to be together, Fräulein," he said. "Away from places like Valhalla, where there is mistrust and suspicion and sometimes even hatred. To be together up there, the man painting and the girl admiring what he does—that can only be good for you both."

I rewarded him with a smile as the jeep started again. "You seem to take your guard duties very seriously, Sergeant."

"Is there any other way to take them, Fräulein? I have known people who did not take such things seriously. Today, they're no longer alive."

"But surely, you don't think . . ."

He shook his head. "I made a promise to Herr Richter once a long time ago, Fräulein," he said in a quiet voice. "I was a soldier of the Wehrmacht, and a good one, but I got into trouble with the authorities. It was nothing I did, it was because my family were Jewish. We had worked for Herr Richter in his factories, all of us, before the war. Someone betrayed us. Herr Richter interceded on our behalf, a dangerous thing to do, but he did it successfully. I was returned to my regiment. My family—my father, my mother, my two sisters— went back to their workbenches in Herr Richter's factory. We were one of the few Jewish families who survived the war as a complete family unit without hurt. When he asked me would I come to America with him and act as his personal guard, I promised him he would be safe while I lived."

"And you have kept him safe," I said. "I admire your loyalty, Sergeant. Loyalty is a rare thing."

"So is talent, Fräulein. Your friend Herr Byron has talent. I saw the sketch, and it is very good. My own son is an artist back in Germany. I learned such things from my son." Paternal pride showed in his voice. "I will be going back to Germany to my son and his family very soon now. This is a good thing for a lonely man."

I smiled. "How do you equate this with your loyalty to Herr Richter, Sergeant?"

Briefly he looked shocked. "I would not leave him while he lives! *Never*!"

"I was joking, Sergeant," I assured him quickly. "Not doubting you."

"The sons, the cousin, they are not like Johann Richter, Fräulein!" he said vehemently. "Have you not noticed that? Have you not read of this in his memoirs? There is only one Johann Richter. When he dies, and he must soon, my loyalty to the Richter family dies with him. It is then I will return to my son! Not before."

"I understand, Sergeant," I said. "I like him too, now that I am beginning to know him better."

"That is why you work so hard," he said. "So we have something in common, you and I." He smiled, pleased. We were turning into the side-track. He added for my protection, "You must hang on when we start to climb. But there is no danger. I know the track, and so does your young friend, who has obligingly left us his tracks to follow."

The sidetrack bounced the jeep, its chains rattling; then we were turning out of it, following Rick's fresh tracks. There were no other tracks once we left the cliff road. The jeep's nose seemed to point up into the air, and we were climbing.

"The night I came here, Paul walked to Connell the chauffeur's house," I said. "I expected to see tracks, and the house." I could see nothing but the small empty valley carpeted with snow.

"You will see the Connell house when you reach the top," he said. "It's far back. Connell has his own road to the house. If he drives to the village, he goes by the cliff road. Nobody uses the sidetrack. Hang on, now—here we go."

The jeep bounced, climbing steeply. We roared over a crest onto a small snow-clad tableland. The air was colder here, the wind stronger. I turned my head, staring down.

"I see the Connell house, I think. But it's almost in the grounds of Valhalla. Paul might as well have walked to the house."

"I wondered about that myself," he said. "When the maid told me what happened. Connell would have taken the battery to the Valhalla garages. Not to his house." He broke off. "Strange, I can't see Herr Byron. He was here painting when I saw him last. You see? There are the marks of the easel, footprints, the tire marks of his car."

"You said there was another way down."

"There is. But I didn't expect him to know it. And the tracks are following the edge." He jerked his head right, away from the brink of the cliff where Rick had been painting the wild sea. "There are some bad places where he is going. Deep drifts in weather like this. Places where the edge sometimes crumbles. Landslides that fall on the road at the Devil's Bend are not uncommon."

He turned the jeep, following Rick's tracks but keeping prudently farther away from the cliff. I began to feel frightened. Not for us but for Rick. It must be hundreds of feet down to the sea! The wind sweeping up the cliff face was damp and salty. The jeep crawled, searching. . . .

"My binoculars are in the glove compartment," Sergeant Freich said. "Adjust them and see if you can find him. The other track goes down from the opposite end of this plateau. Can you see anything there?"

Focusing quickly, I stared through the powerful lenses. "Nothing!"

"Keep searching, Fräulein. If you see the truck he came in headed down, we have nothing to worry about. He has finished his painting and is going home."

"He paints slowly," I muttered. "And the light is still good. He would not be going home yet. He . . ." I broke off. "I think I just saw something go over the edge where you said! Something just disappeared. . . . It's gone now!"

"Good!" he said. "He finished his work and is on his way home! I too was becoming concerned about him. But you and I can now return by the way we came. It makes no difference to me, and you will not have so far to walk." The jeep began to turn, moving back toward where we had come up.

"Wait!" I cried. The level ground around us was like the tabletop of some California mesa, and there were trees growing at the edge of the high ground. Trees deformed by wind and salt spray, trees leaning away landward from their bitter torment. Frozen snow decorated their branches with stalactite icicles that made it difficult for me to see past them. But there was movement in among them. I was sure of it. Something, a vehicle of some kind, was moving parallel with the top of the cliff. It appeared to be descending, for the effect from where I watched through binoculars was as though it was submerging, sinking gradually from sight.

I thrust the binoculars into Sergeant Freich's hand. "Take them! Quickly, Sergeant! Look where you said the track leads down."

The jeep stopped abruptly as he lifted the glasses, peering through.

"See it?" I asked anxiously.

"I saw *something*!" he muttered. "It's gone now. It could have been Herr Byron."

"I saw him up here earlier, as I told you, Sergeant. I saw him quite clearly. He was driving a dirty off-white pickup truck. It was open at the back and had low sides. I could see his gear in the back. He borrows it from one of the Fifeness fishermen. What I just saw and you just saw was dark in color and much smaller. It wasn't the pickup. It couldn't have been. It looked more like this jeep to me, and it was about the same color—olive green."

He scowled at me. Like someone given unpleasant information. "You are sure, Fräulein?"

"Yes, I am! Don't you agree?"

"I do not wish to agree," he muttered. "But that is another thing. Because now I must try to find out who it is who knows the existence of these tracks other than Herr Byron and myself."

He smiled grimly and thrust the binoculars into my hands. The jeep accelerated, and we went clanking through the crust of ice toward the opposite side of the clifftop. I raised the binoculars to my eyes quickly, searching, but whoever I had glimpsed there was gone now. There must be tracks over there, though. Someone like Sergeant Freich should be able to tell by the treads what kind of vehicle it was, even if we could not see it again.

We had followed Rick's tracks quite a distance and were turning away from them now. We must have followed them without noticing that a second vehicle had followed carefully in Rick's tracks before us. I frowned into the binoculars. How could we have missed noticing that a second set of tracks diverged from those of Rick's truck?

That was impossible.

Therefore the strange vehicle must have climbed to the clifftop from the direction of Fifeness village. The Valhalla jeeps were all the same color, olive green. But if the other vehicle I'd glimpsed was from Valhalla, why had it gone so far out of its way to reach the clifftop? I was remembering that Rick had been nonchalantly painting up here in full view of Valhalla windows. Anybody down there could have seen him.

I was afraid suddenly, remembering the jealous hatred in Paul Richter's blue eyes. Paul had gone to the village, Adrienne had told me. The vehicle I'd just glimpsed could have been one of the Valhalla olive-green jeeps driven by Paul Richter.

Where was Rick?

I swung the binoculars in an arc, searching the high ground ahead and to our right where the trees grew the thickest. They thinned toward the cliff edge above the Devil's Bend.

"Sergeant, does the trail down come out between the Devil's Bend and the village?"

"Yes. The Devil's Bend is directly ahead now, just beyond where the trees end. Why?"

"If we could see Rick painting above the Devil's Bend, as we did from Valhalla, he could see us?"

"All the way from Valhalla to the Connells' road. And again once we reached the crest here. He'd see us now—if he was still up here."

"But anyone coming from the village and driving up the other track? He couldn't see them, could he? They could drive through the trees behind him unseen?"

"They could, no doubt. But we would see them once we reached the crest above Connells' road. We could see the vehicle and whoever was in it. But there is no sign of anyone."

"But not if they saw us first and stayed back where the trees are thickest. Then they could turn back and go down the way they came up, without being seen by us at all. The way we saw that other vehicle starting down . . ." I broke off suddenly, concentrating, sick with apprehension. "Sergeant, look! Near the edge of the cliff!"

"Verdammt!" he muttered. "Why didn't I think of this sooner?"

The jeep turned, picking up speed, while I tried to steady the binoculars on the dark shadow on the snow near the trees. A shadow that was beginning to take shape, to become the body of a man lying on his back, one arm extended over the head that lolled sideways at the end of a deep furrow in the snow, irregular footmarks. . . .

"It's Rick!" I cried, shocked.

I was out and running as the jeep skidded to a stop. I fell on my knees beside him. "Rick, are you all right? Rick? I was unable to suppress a sob in my voice.

"Let me look at him, Fräulein. I have some knowledge of such things." I was being put gently but firmly aside by Sergeant Freich. "He is unconscious but breathing. There is a first-aid box in the back of the jeep—get it."

I nodded through my tears and ran for it. Coming back, I saw blood on Sergeant Freich's big hands. He had turned Rick on his side. He lay without moving, barely breathing. I opened the box with trembling hands and held it ready. "Sergeant, he isn't . . . ?"

"Young men have tough skulls," he muttered, choosing things from the box. "He is probably concussed, but I can find no broken bones, no other injury."

"What do you think happened? Did he fall? Why was he crawling here, toward the edge of the cliff?" I shuddered. This was the Devil's Bend below us. Even at this height above the road and the sea there was the salty moisture of spray in the air, the updraft of cold sea air.

"Crawling?" he muttered.

I glanced back toward the trees, following the deep channel of track through the snow that he had made, to collapse at last with his arm extended toward the abyss no more than a few feet away.

"He must have crawled here from the trees," I said. "He moved from where we saw him painting here on the edge of the cliff this morning. He must have decided to paint the sea from a different angle, toward Valhalla."

"He did not crawl here," Sergeant Freich muttered. "A man hurt as he is does not crawl anywhere."

I glanced back along that furrow in the snow, and stared. Rick's folding chair stood back there in the shadows among the trees, looking lonely without Rick and his easel. The track started there, ended where Rick lay. I saw the easel then, lying flat on the snow.

"He was painting back there among the trees. I can see his folding chair and the easel. But how did he get here?"

"Someone dragged him here by one arm," Sergeant Freich said grimly. "From where the easel is overturned. Someone who came from the other track. Unseen, the way you suggested. One man, who made the footprints in the snow you saw here straddling the furrow where Herr Byron's body was dragged. He walked backward, dragging Herr Byron, who is a heavy young man. Then, when he reached this spot, he saw our jeep coming."

I stared at him. "And ran away? Ran back to where he'd left the jeep, and drove away?"

He nodded. "Which makes your young friend lucky, Fräulein. Since what we interrupted was his intended murder."

"*His murder?*" I gasped.

"Can you think of another reason he could have had to render Herr Byron unconscious by a heavy blow to the back of the head and drag him this close to the edge?"

"I can't believe it!"

He gave me an oddly impatient look. "You can't afford not to believe it, Fräulein!"

He was using some acrid spirit in a glass vial to revive poor Rick, and the smell of it almost took my breath. Rick's hand moved, trying feebly to push it away.

"You think whoever we saw driving in the distance did this to Rick?"

"He seems to be waking," Sergeant Freich muttered, pleased. He withdrew the vial and corked it. "Perhaps he can tell you what happened."

Rick's gray eyes opened. He was moving, trying to sit up. He saw me and stilled. "Lorna?"

"Rick, what happened?"

"What happened?" This time he sat up with

Sergeant Freich's help and looked around, puzzling, his face pale beneath its tan.

"You hurt your head, Herr Byron," Sergeant Freich said. "We found you lying here. You have a bump on your head. Do you know how you got it?"

"I must have fallen . . ." Rick's eyes were still vague and mildly surprised. He put up a weak hand to feel the bandage and winced. "Did I fall? I couldn't have. I was working over there among the trees when I heard your jeep coming. Then . . ."

"Then what, Rick?" I asked.

He shook his head. "I . . . don't remember getting hurt. I was painting!"

"Someone dragged you here, Herr Byron," Sergeant Freich said gruffly. "We found you unconscious, with an injury to the back of your head. Did you see anyone up here other than Fräulein Mitchell and me? Someone who could have hit you from behind?"

"You're kidding, Sergeant!" Rick stared around disbelievingly.

"Rick, please try to remember," I urged him.

Sergeant Freich shook his head, frowning. "If someone stopped a vehicle at the top of the track just out of sight and crept up behind him through the trees, his feet making no sound in the snow, there is nothing for him to remember, Fräulein. But perhaps if I am quick I can still see the vehicle on the road to Fifeness and recognize it. Get him into the jeep when you can. I will not be long away."

For a big man in his late fifties Sergeant Freich was fast. Supporting Rick, I watched him run to the jeep for the field glasses. He had dragged something else from a leather sheath on the driver's side. A deadly-looking rifle with a telescopic sight. With glasses and rifle he plunged in among the trees through the snow.

Rick was lolling in my arms. He was conscious, but vague and still dazed. He muttered something that didn't make sense. Urging him to cooperate, I got him onto his feet and into Sergeant Freich's jeep. Not long after that, Sergeant Freich returned breathlessly, shaking his head.

"He was not in sight!" he said. "Either I was too slow or he drove off the road somewhere below here. How is Herr Byron now?"

"He seems still dazed."

"Can you drive the jeep? We must get him to Dr. Brewster in Fifeness."

I told him I had driven jeeps in California. But it was a hair-raising drive down to the cliff road. It started snowing again, covering the tracks of men and vehicles. I could not have done it except that the sergeant drove the truck slowly ahead, and he had strapped a drowsy and semiconscious Rick into the seat next to mine.

Dr. Brewster examined Rick and told us Sergeant Freich had done about all that could be done. He gave Rick a shot to make him sleep, and an antibiotic. We took him home to the widow Clout's, who fussed about him kindly. I had an hour with Rick before Sergeant Freich finished his business in town and called back for me. By then Rick was fast asleep.

I had lost most of the afternoon. I worked late that night.

★ 8 ★

Rick did not come to work the next day, Tuesday. Herr Richter returned to work, but he did not look well. His face seemed colorless, the lines of pain and illness more apparent. Adrienne confided that he was losing weight at an alarming rate and Dr. Brewster wanted to send him to some famous cancer clinic in Boston, but he had refused. He wanted only one thing, he told Dr. Brewster: to live long enough to complete the book. She added, resentfully I thought, that he told Brewster that might be sooner than expected—thanks to me.

She said Herman was furious when she told him, and she supposed Paul would feel the same way. News, it seemed, traveled fast in Valhalla. Especially when it was supposed to be kept secret. I was glad the slip had come from Johann and not from Rick or me. Johann must have still been in the grip of whatever painkilling drugs Dr. Brewster had fed him on the weekend.

The police came to Valhalla that day, sent on the widow Clout's insistence when she had learned what happened. They talked to Sergeant

140

Freich and me separately. I told them the truth as
I saw it, and so, I believe, did Sergeant Freich.
They had a few words with Johann before leaving, but he could tell them nothing. Sheriff Walton, the officer in charge, told me that the snowfall
the day before had made conditions impossible for
them. They had found nothing to indicate who
Rick's assailant had been. Rick could not help
them; he hadn't seen his attacker.

They had no clues, nothing to go on except the
testimony of Hans Freich and me. And our testimony, he told me bluntly, identified neither the
vehicle we claimed to have seen nor the person or
persons in it.

I couldn't deny that. It was disappointing, but
at least Sheriff Walton tried. He said that it could
have been a drifter, someone who owned a jeep.
Though muggings were still relatively uncommon
in the Maine countryside, it was not unheard of.
He added for my information that the Richters
were not the only people who owned olive-green
jeeps. The armed forces had been painting their
jeeps olive green ever since they were first manufactured for World War Two. And these jeeps often ended up being sold as used vehicles, for
general use, still of the same color.

Even the sheriff's office, he confided, bought
jeeps every now and then for rough work in the
area, and though they bought them new, they too
were always olive green.

But Sheriff Walton was a conscientious police
officer, for after he had questioned us upstairs he
repeated the process downstairs. He asked every-

one from Erma Richter down to the chauffeur and maids which members of the Valhalla household had been away from the house at the approximate time Rick was attacked. The only other absentee, of course, was Paul Richter. The sheriff came back the next day to question Paul.

Paul was furious that he should even be questioned, Herman told Adrienne. Paul threatened to sue the sheriff for defamation, and the sheriff threatened to subpoena Paul. Adrienne said they parted enemies. But nothing came of their threats, except mutual dislike.

Johann, Sergeant Freich, Bruno, and I went back to work. So too did Rick Byron, now totally absorbed in his work and reluctant to miss a sitting.

The second sketch began to take shape, much improved, I thought, over the first. Johann liked it too, and Sergeant Freich confided to me one day through our closed-circuit television that his son couldn't have done better. The second sketch in oils, we both agreed, had caught Johann's stern expression exactly. There didn't seem the need for another. But the second was no sooner completed than Rick started on a third.

And now as I worked on the translation of Johann's Richter's memoirs, I was beginning to realize that Johann's sons might indeed have reason to fear what their father might write. The scene in the memoirs was changing. It had moved to Berlin, where Johann was becoming involved for business reasons, industrially and socially, with the tight circle of people supporting the hierarchy of the National Socialist Party. As a leading industrialist who at least gave lip service to the Nazis, he began to receive lucrative contracts.

Soon Johann was accepted as a wealthy and generous friend of the party. Hitler had become chancellor, and with the death of Hindenburg, dictator. The rape of Europe began.

Johann's involvement with the Nazis had been apparent from the beginning, though it seemed a business rather than a personal involvement. But suddenly, with the approach of war, a new factor began to appear. For Paul, too, was becoming at least a satellite of the movement. Johann was beginning to mention his son Paul, the brilliant student, more as a young stormtrooper patriot. I was becoming more and more absorbed in the memoirs as they concerned the emerging Paul Richter.

I worked on to the beginning of the war. Paul Richter was called up. Johann wanted him released from military duties to complete his studies in industrial chemistry and go to work in the Richter chemistry manufacturing complex, but suddenly Paul wanted only to be a soldier. It would have been easy for Johann, through his influential friends, to keep his son with him, as other wealthy friends of the Nazi hierarchy were doing. But Johann was powerless against the fervent patriotism of his elder son.

The moment Johann gave in to his son, it seemed to me, was the moment Paul's personal involvement with the Nazis began.

Paul's connection with the party, at first an unwilling one undertaken only because of his father's business association with the Nazis, was beginning to change as time passed. Reading and translating, I noticed the reluctance had become willingness to participate, quickly changing to *enthusiasm*, as his father's wealth and influence ensured Paul's rapid promotion. Paul seemed rapidly acquiring a taste for power and the fringe benefits that were coming his way as a loyal friend of the Nazi hierarchy.

Johann hinted with disgust at bacchanalian orgies held by high government officials, some homosexual, in which his son took part. Paul acquired a lovely mistress, then several. Johann cut off his allowance, but wrote bitterly that this made little difference, as his son now seemed to have more money than he did. Although officially Paul was still a soldier now with the rank of captain, he seemed to have no military duties.

Then, as I read on, Paul was transferred abruptly to Himmler's elite SS. He had become Major Paul Richter, working on some top-secret project that Johann appared to know very little about except that it entailed the building of a factory which resembled a fortress, closely guarded by Paul's own company of SS troops.

A few chapters farther on, I discovered Paul surfacing again as his father's principal source of worry. Paul, now Colonel Paul Richter, had become the commandant in complete charge of a project that involved the manufacture of top-secret chemicals and gases. Paul was now pressuring his father into supplying the basic chemical

elements from his Stuttgart factories. He was accusing Johann of shielding and employing non-
Aryan workers.

The chapter ended with Johann's refusal and
an appeal to his friends in the party to help him.

His powerful friends, though, proved less powerful than his son Paul. For though Johann wrote
that the people under his protection were now
safe, there was an admission that he was now supplying under duress the basic elements to what he
called "Paul's research laboratories."

I found myself wondering if the people he re-
ferred to as now being safe were Sergeant Hans
Freich and his family. I decided this might explain Sergeant Freich's remark to me that when
Johann died his loyalty to the Richter family
would die with Johann, for the sons were not as
the father.

I shivered, reading. They were not, indeed! I
was finding that thought more and more frightening. A man who would betray his own father to
the Nazis for sheltering people like Hans Freich
would stop at nothing now if he thought himself
threatened by what I was reading. And the
memoirs were becoming a very real threat to
Paul. My fear grew as I thought about that. Paul's
resentment of me seemed becoming more intense
all the time. A part of that, I realized, was because
he was a lonely and jealous man who found me attractive. But there was more to it than that.
There had to be. His hatred and suspicion of the
memoirs were becoming paranoid. It showed
whenever we sat together at table in the Richter

dining room and he looked at Johann or me with uncompromising malice in his blue eyes. There was hatred in his voice too.

It seemed to me Paul feared the memoirs only because he was a guilty man. His guilt grew deeper, stronger as I translated each chapter, each page of the memoirs of Johann Richter.

What Johann was writing was the simple truth. This was the way it had been with his son Paul in the war years. This was what Paul Richter had known and feared his father would write. Truth that Paul would do anything to destroy.

Paul had to stop the publication of the memoirs, because Paul, not his father, was the war criminal. I remembered Paul on the cliff road that night near the Devil's Bend. If I had blundered to my death in the terrifying darkness and the gale, Johann would have had to start again to search for a translator and secretary whom he could trust. This would have taken time, possibly a long time. In his condition it would have been almost certain that Johann would not live to complete his memoirs.

Paul had meant to murder me that night! It was a horrifying realization. But Paul had never intended even to leave it to chance for the gale to hurl me into the wild sea. He had meant to do that himself. Paul was the dark figure I had seen stalking the jeep from behind, where I would least expect him. I knew now that there was a path by which Paul could have approached the jeep from the direction of the village.

And as I thought of this, horrified, a new terror

presented itself. Sergeant Freich had been surprised that anyone other than Rick and he knew
of the existence of that other track. He had tried
to find out who the other man was. I knew the answer to that now—Paul Richter. That had to be
Paul driving a Valhalla jeep that the sergeant and
I glimpsed through the trees. Paul, I realized with
sick fear, had been trying to murder Rick as he
had tried to murder me, to prevent the completion of the cover painting and delay the completion of the book.

It was only through blind luck that either of us
had survived. I by running from him in terror,
Rick because Sergeant Freich and I had appeared
when Paul least expected interference. It was
clear that Paul would do anything to prevent his
father from completing his memoirs.

And Johann Richter might still not live to finish them, I was realizing in increasing fear. For
the one sure way left for Paul now was for Paul
himself to end his father's life.

Perhaps before this the thought of patricide had
been repugnant to Paul. Though he had shown
no compunction about attempting to murder Rick
and me. But that might not be so any longer. Not
if he realized how quickly the work on the
memoirs was progressing now, thanks to my ingenuity. And if Adrienne had told Herman about
that, Paul must know it too.

Paul could not afford to wait, if he knew that.
Paul had to kill Johann before what Johann wrote
became irreversibly damaging to him. I had no
doubt of Paul's guilt during the war or now. But

as I thought back over what Johann had written, there was nothing specific to say what Paul was doing in his laboratories, other than that it was the manufacture of chemicals and gases. So far, apparently, Johann did not know. I wondered if Paul had reasoned that this was the way it must be in the memoirs. After all, Paul had lived these events. Paul knew.

Was Paul waiting, knowing that whatever evil purpose his research served could be revealed only in the final chapters? Of late I had noticed that Johann was no longer using his faded notebooks; he was writing from memory, no longer asking me to check dates. He was writing as though everything that happened then was indelibly recorded in his memory. I had not reached any of that spontaneous material yet. Each night he locked it carefully in the wall safe from which each morning he removed the pages of my new day's work and gave them to me.

But soon now, within days perhaps, I would be reading and translating the pages of those final chapters.

I glanced at the clock. Rick was working on the portrait inside. They were having a long sitting in the inner room, the longest yet. Listening, I could hear the occasional murmur of their deep male voices. Rick's German was improving; he learned quickly, I had discovered, and Johann clearly enjoyed talking with him when he wasn't busy checking my work. Rick and I hadn't been alone together in days, but even then he had told me that the portrait was going well and he would soon be finished.

They were working under lights in there, and I had forgotten to turn mine on. I got up wearily and switched on the desk lamp. I sat down again but found I could no longer work. I was too worried by what I had read. I wanted to talk about it to Johann Richter—but how to tell him that I suspected his elder and favorite son of planning to murder him? Yet I had to tell someone, to ask advice in a situation beyond my youthful comprehension. Murder was something you read about in books of fiction, or saw in films, that kept you awake or woke you in fright. Murder was not for real, except in newspapers.

They were coming from the inner rooms of Johann's suite. I heard Johann say something, and Rick's pleased laughter. I bent to tap the keys, and misspelled the word, something I rarely did.

Maybe I should tell Sergeant Freich. Rick was smiling at me as he put down his gear near the outer door. *Rick.* I could tell Rick. I must tell Rick. He would know what I should do.

"Why so grim, Lorna?" Rick asked. "Tired?"

"A little," I admitted.

"Of course she is tired," Johann said. "She works hard and well. Without her help these things might not have been possible." He was studying my face, frowning slightly. "She does not often make mistakes or need to rewrite, as I frequently do. Do you know what day tomorrow is, Fräulein?"

I stared at him, puzzling. "Tomorrow?" The days passed so quickly.

"No, don't look for your calendar, Fräulein," he said, smiling. "It is my rest day tomorrow. Sunday. And I intend to rest."

"I'll work tomorrow and catch up some more pages."

He shook his head. "It is three weeks since you had a rest. As you once told me, so I now tell you, that you will work the better for it next week. There is a dance tonight in the village, Herr Byron tells me, and he has something to celebrate tonight."

"Oh?" I glanced at Rick, but found no help there. He was just grinning at me.

"He has completed the portrait, and it is very good," Johann said. "But you shall see it for yourself. And Hans." He raised his voice and looked at the television set. "Hans, come here. I have something I want you to see."

I got up quickly to congratulate Rick, and he gave me a peck on the cheek, awkwardly, because Johann was watching with sly humor in his cold blue eyes. Across the passage Hans was putting Bruno on guard in his absence.

"Now there only remain the last two chapters, Fräulein," Johann said. "You and I will have something to celebrate than, ja?"

Sergeant Freich came in as Rick opened the door, and we went in through the library to view the portrait.

I heard Sergeant Freich's quick, surprised breath as he saw it. "He paints like a Holbein,

Herr Richter!" he said approvingly. "I did not know there were those who could portray character in this style in America." He shook his head. "It is you, Herr Richter, it *is* you."

Johann was smiling and nodding approvingly. "I like it," he said. "Yes, I like it. What do you think, Fräulein?"

"I think it's great," I murmured admiringly, and noticed Rick's pleased smile. There was a similarity to a portrait by Holbein the Younger that I'd seen in a famous German gallery. Johann's stern, austere face looked back at me unsmiling from the canvas, the blue eyes slightly narrowed. There was a difference between man and portrait, though. I puzzled, trying to define it.

I decided Rick had painted a slightly younger man, as he had told me he would. The ravages of disease were not quite as apparent in the portrait as they were today. The pain, the worry, the lines of despair, the pallor, all seemed less. Because of this, the true character of Johann Richter showed through more clearly. The strength, the determination, the moral courage, were all there abundantly. Rick had painted Johann as he must have been a few years ago, before leaving Germany.

This was not the Johann Richter of today. This man I could readily imagine interceding on behalf of the Freich family. Or refusing to let his factories be used for the production of deadly chemicals and gases that might be used against his fellow men.

"And now, Herr Byron," Johann said cheerfully, "you and I have a little business transaction to complete. I have a check to write for you, and my thanks go with it."

As we followed him back into the office, Rick said in a low voice, "You heard what the man said—you deserve the day off tomorrow. Are you going to help me celebrate? The widow will be glad to have you after the dance tonight. I'll drive you back tomorrow."

"Well . . ." I hesitated. With the end of the memoirs so close, I wanted to work on. I wanted to finish the job and leave this place. But my fear was still strong. I needed someone to whom I could confide my troubles and suspicions. I needed to talk to Rick about these things, and Johann was offering me this chance to be alone with him. . . .

He said, starting to frown, "I thought you'd be as pleased as I am."

Hesitating, I weakened and agreed. "I am, Rick. And I need to talk to you. I need a friend. Okay, I'll go upstairs for my things. Can I change at widow Clout's?"

"Of course. The widow likes you. She's always asking about you."

I put my work away, covered my typewriter, and dashed upstairs. When I came back, Sergeant Freich was back at his post, and an off-duty Bruno was sleeping blissfully with his head resting on the toe of Sergeant Freich's highly polished shoe, which, I noticed, the sergeant was being careful not to move, lest he wake him. Through Sergeant Freich's television I watched Rick shake hands with Johann Richter and Johann let him out.

Bruno stirred conscientiously and opened one eye to see what was happening, even though officially he was not on guard. He recognized Rick and me, his tail twitched in a minuscule wag of recognition, and his eye closed again.

We met Adrienne as we came downstairs, and I told her where I was going. She had begun to accept that I really disliked Paul, and she knew me well enough to realize I was falling in love with Rick. Sometimes I thought she had known that even before I did. She merely shrugged now, accepting whatever I told her. The spontaneity had gone from our once-close friendship.

But she couldn't resist saying, "Poor Paul is in his laboratory. Herman and I haven't seen much of him for days. I think he's lonely." She ran her eyes over Rick and sniffed disparagingly, making a comparison, I knew. "Oh, well," she added resignedly. "Have fun. . . ."

"I mean to," I told her resentfully.

"What was that about with Adrienne?" Rick asked suspiciously when we had settled into the pickup truck. "She thinks Paul Richter is lonely—but says for you to have fun? Does she think that guy has some sort of claim on you, Lorna?"

Another jealous man, I couldn't stand! I shook my head. "No way! I've told you I don't like Paul. I didn't think you'd need to ask."

He frowned. "Okay, I'm sorry, Lorna. But you said there was something you needed to talk to me about, and when she said that about Paul . . ." He hesitated awkwardly. "I thought maybe you . . ."

He saw my expression and shrugged guiltily. "Okay, I said I'm sorry!"

"You should be!" I said bitterly. "I did want to talk to you. And it is about Paul!" I stopped him with a gesture as he started to protest. "No, wait! Paul Richter is the last man on earth I'd ever want to be involved with."

He shook his head angrily. "Has he offended you, Lorna?"

Offended me? That made me smile. I began to tell him. We were close to the sidetrack to the Connell house, and he pulled in off the cliff road to stare at me, at first disbelieving, then shocked, as he listened. I watched his astonishment change to cold fury as I told him for the first time what had happened at the Devil's Bend and of my suspicion that it was Paul who had dragged him almost to the edge of the cliff and his death.

"Does this have something to do with the memoirs?" he demanded.

"He doesn't want them published, I know that. I think he will do anything to prevent his father finishing them. As he tried to stop me from translating them, and you from painting the portrait. He did these things to cost his father time, knowing he doesn't have long to live."

"What's in the memoirs to drive him to murder?" he asked grimly. "It must be something incriminating?"

"I agreed not to speak of the contents to anyone, Rick. So I can't, not even to you. But I haven't read anything yet that could be really incriminating to Paul, but I am expecting to."

"What about the others? Erma? Herman? Johann himself?"

"No. But Paul has to be guilty of something. . . ."

"I heard Johann say you had only two chapters to go." He frowned. "Paul must believe it will be in the final chapters."

"I feel that he knows it will be there! He knows his father. He knows the only way to stop Johann is to kill him."

"Or you," Rick muttered, looking at me. He bent forward, starting the jeep again. "You're not going back to Valhalla!" he said, fiercely protective.

I smiled affectionately. "Rick, don't be ridiculous! I work there, and I need the money. You got your check today, and I don't get mine until the memoirs are completed."

"We can do without it," he said. "We'll go to Boston, where my folks live. I can get all the portrait commissions I can paint in Boston. Too many! That was why I came to Maine, to broaden my concept of painting."

"We? You're talking as though we were married."

He looked at me steadily for a long moment. "Because that's what I want," he said. "Don't you?"

I was staring at him blankly, yet I knew there was no reason for me to be bewildered by what he'd said. I think I'd known that was the way it would be with us ever since I walked downhill through the blizzard with Rick toward the widow

Clout's house in Fifeness village. And if his proposal wasn't quite worded the way I would have expected, what did that matter?

"Yes . . ." I admitted softly.

For a while after that neither of us said much of anything, except the kinds of things people say at such times. Reluctantly I began to reason again. Calming Rick, I assured him that it was Johann Richter who was in danger. Not me. The memoirs were too near completion for any injury to me, the translator, to stop them now.

"I wouldn't want anything to happen to the old man," he said, frowning as he considered that. "He sort of grows on you."

"He has Hans Freich to protect him," I said. "It was Hans who saved you, remember? And then, there's Bruno. Rick, I'm going to stay at Valhalla until the manuscript is completed. I'll leave this place forever the day it's finished. I promise."

"Not without me," he said. "Okay. We won't let this thing spoil our weekend."

"I had to tell someone," I said. "I can't talk to Adrienne anymore. She's changed. I thought of telling Sergeant Freich, but . . ."

He turned the pickup into the cliff road. "If Hans suspected trouble, he would be even more alert. Okay, tell him. I'll talk to Sheriff Walton. He's a good cop. He'll tell us what to do."

"I've been so frightened, Rick!" I muttered. "I had to tell you."

"Try to forget it," he said seriously. "Do you know, this is the first weekend of spring? And Johann gave me this . . ." He fumbled for the check and showed it to me, with the wind flapping it about.

"Five hundred dollars!" I said admiringly. "Put it down quickly, before the wind blows it away."

"Look again," he said, grinning.

I caught his hand and steadied the check. It was on the Portland National Bank for . . . I looked again, and stared, wide-eyed.

"Five *thousand* dollars?" I gasped. "You asked that much?"

"You think it too much? That maybe I should give it back?"

Now I have offended him, I thought, dismayed! "Rick, the painting's great!" I muttered in confusion.

"I didn't ask for that, *he* offered it." He chuckled unexpectedly, and when I looked at him, he was not angry, but amused. "He knows he could sell it for that or more tomorrow. It's below the average price for a Byron portrait. I didn't want his commission or his money, but I'm glad now that I accepted, because that gave me you. I like the fringe benefit. The money doesn't matter." He glanced at me sidelong. "There's a lot you don't know about me, darling."

I sighed and moved closer. "I think I already know all I need to know about you, Rick!" I murmured contentedly.

★ 9 ★

The first week of spring was beautiful. The winter chill seemed gone. There was even a glimpse of the green burgeoning of leaf buds on the old chestnut tree beneath my window. But the second week of spring began with scudding clouds from the northeast. The chill of winter returned. The strengthening wind became colder and colder. As the widow Clout said when we met, it was as though it came via the north pole.

Snow came with it, and the inevitable bitter rain and sleet, until it was as bad as the weather I'd encountered when I first came to Valhalla. I caught up with my work; there was nothing else to do, with the weather as it was. The lights failed twice in that week, and the grim weather seemed to be affecting Johann's health badly.

He gave me the second-to-last chapter of his memoirs at the beginning of the second week of spring. I began work on it, enthralled and shocked. Paul was ordered to Poland to a town called Zabrze. Johann quarreled bitterly with his son, not wanting him to go there. Johann did not say why, but soon an infamous name began to appear among Paul's friends and superior officers in Poland. Adolf Eichmann! That night when I worked alone in the study I checked the town of Zabrze in the adjoining library.

"Zabrze," I read. "City in southwest Poland, 100 miles southeast of Wroclaw." Not that that meant anything to me. But it had coal mines and steel mills, and its products included machinery, glass, and chemicals. That figured, I realized. Paul's top-secret chemical-research plants were being moved to Zabrze on the direct order of Himmler, and Paul with them. Johann wrote with relief that he was no longer required to supply Paul with basic chemicals. Whatever experiments Paul was carrying out would now be supplied from Zabrze factories.

Johann was off the hook, but his worry about Paul was apparent in every page. Johann wrote now what he would have been afraid to put into words then, that he believed the war lost and final defeat certain. Paul's mysterious research was being linked vaguely with infamous names—Eichmann, Heydrich, Kaltenbrunner . . .

There were conferences in Berlin with Himmler, and at Krakow, in Poland. But other events were concerning Johann. The Stuttgart factories were bombed and gutted. He wrote that Hans Freich, now a sergeant in the Wehrmacht, had been decorated for outstanding bravery during the Normandy invasion. Johann himself was working beside rescuers and survivors searching for casualties and bodies among the wreckage.

Hans Freich's family were first missing, then confirmed dead.

The chapter ended on a grim note; the Allied noose was tightening around the Germany of the Third Reich. The Russians were poised to invade Poland; German armies were preparing to fight within Germany itself, with Allied troops already within a few miles of the border at Aachen. Paul had moved to some Polish town called Oswiecim. And suddenly then there was no more about Colonel Paul Richter. No more at all! It was as though, like Hans Freich's family, he too was dead.

I finished the chapter late at night, and was forced to wait until next day before I could read the climactic final pages. Johann was still working when I finished, and no persuasion of mine could stop him. When I asked wearily if I too could continue with the early pages of the new chapter he was completing, he gave me a curt no and went on typing feverishly.

Johann was missing at breakfast, and I was not surprised when an obviously worried Hans Freich told me the old man had worked all night and Erma Richter, in panic, had phoned Dr. Brewster. From the sound of the weather outside, it seemed unlikely Dr. Brewster could reach Valhalla. Conditions were worsening; we could barely see out the windows. The temperature had fallen below zero, and there was snow and ice everywhere. Wind howled around the great house, peppering the ice-coated windows with sleet. And Johann had done something he never had done before, I

saw as I entered the study. A folder waited for me
on my desk, my day's work, the last chapter. Usually he had to open the wall safe to get it for me,
but he had not taken any risk, I decided as I
looked around. He must have left for his bedroom
only minutes before I arrived for work. Coffee on
his desk was still warm in a cup he had only
sipped.

I hurried preparing for the day's work, fighting
an impulse to first skim through the climax to my
months of work, as I remembered that I was on
camera in the closed-circuit television that was
part of Johann's security system. He could be
watching me from his bedroom, as Hans was from
his guardroom.

Forcing myself to be patient, I prepared for the
day before I sat down to open the folder and type
the first page. I stared at the chapter heading, surprised. "Epilogue," I read.

"You are surprised, Fräulein?" I started as
Johann Richter's tired voice spoke to me from the
study television set. "Press the red button on your
desk, please, and I will explain."

I pressed obediently, cutting us off from the
guardroom, and he continued, "What I have given
you to work on today is not the final chapter you
expected, but an epilogue written some time ago.
It describes the trial and my exoneration. I committed no crime against humanity, unless it is a
crime to be loyal to your country. I had no politics
other than that. I have written my memoirs to
vindicate the decision of Nuremberg that I was
personally blameless. But there were others who

were not, and should be punished. Some, like Eich-mann, escaped to South America. Others, because of lack of evidence, were never charged. In the last chapter I write of these things. Sparing nobody, Fräulein. It is probable that some of the men I write of will be deported, to be tried and punished in Germany, where their crimes were committed."

I frowned at the television set from which his weary face watched me. "How does this concern me, Herr Richter?"

"Such knowledge could be dangerous to you, even in America," he said grimly. "Though in Germany today, so long after the commission of the crimes, charges laid and punishments given are lighter. I do not want you to know what I write, until the book is published. Understand?"

I shrugged. "Yes. But how will you cope with the translation and typing?"

"With your help, as it was in the beginning," he said. "Except that instead of giving you the page to correct, I will give you the single word, or the sentence, of which I am doubtful. I have no difficulty with names, which will be omitted. If the typing of the last chapter is not what the publishers expect, let them have it retyped. Agreed?"

"Yes."

"Then the memoirs will be completed and on the way to the publishers within a week. We shall have something to celebrate that night, even if the others do not know it. You will be there, of course."

"Of course."

"Then that's settled," he said. "I am very tired, but I will be back at work after lunch. Good night, Fräulein."

"Good night, Herr Richter."

The screen went blank.

The week passed slowly. The epilogue was not on the level of interest to me personally that the preceding chapters had been. It dealt with the occupation, the preliminary investigation, the trial, and the dismissal of the charges against Johann. I hardly saw Paul that week. Adrienne said he was working all day in his laboratory on some project Herman didn't know about. Johann pored over his final chapter, writing and rewriting. We both were working far too hard, but it was as though we had tapped a hidden reserve of strength needed for the final drive.

I reached the last pages of the epilogue before Johann finished his chapter. They dealt with the migration to America, as Johann Richter put it: "So that someday my family can be reunited there, with whatever debts any one of us may have owed society paid, and their bitter memories put behind us for all time."

The final sentence of that last page concluded: "It is as good as done; Paul has agreed to join us there from Argentina."

I frowned as I typed beneath that line the words I'd been wanting to type for months: "The End."

I puzzled over that for the rest of the day, while I helped with the translation of words and sentences for Johann. There had been no mention in anything I'd read about Paul going to Argentina. The reason for that must be contained in the last chapter that Johann didn't want me to read.

But I could find no clue to that in the individual words, phrases, or sentences without any proper names that I was translating. I had read the evidence given by Johann at his trial in the epilogue. Johann had said nothing there that could possibly incriminate anyone else, including Paul. His answers had seemed truthful and direct. They had impressed me with his honesty, as they must have impressed the judges who summarily dismissed the charges against him without hearing the scores of people wanting to testify that he had kept them safe from persecution in his Stuttgart factories.

Waiting for work now, I remembered that Paul had been connected with Adolf Eichmann in some way, and Eichmann had successfully fled to Argentina, where he remained hidden until kidnapped by Israelis and tried and hanged for mass murder.

I discovered Johann Richter smiling at me wearily. "It is done," he said. "It is done at last, Fräulein!"

"Congratulations!" I smiled, and received a peck on the cheek from dry and withered lips.

"I have never been so weary," he muttered. "So we will hold a little dinner tonight, while I am able to enjoy it." He glanced up at the television set. "Hans, come in here, old friend! You must share a glass of wine with us."

He brought champagne from an inner room, opened it himself, and poured three glasses while we waited for Sergeant Freich to rearrange the guard and open the door. Sergeant Freich came in, glancing curiously from one of us to the other as he took his glass.

"To the only two people in this great house whom I can trust!" Johann Richter toasted. "With my thanks and gratitude. *Prosit!*"

Sergeant Richter's expression changed. "It is finished, then, mein Herr?" he asked with satisfaction when we had sipped.

"It is finished, Hans. Tonight I will celebrate at dinner, proclaiming to them all that it is over. That I have accomplished what I set out to do so long ago."

The sergeant frowned at his glass. "Is this wise, mein Herr?"

Johann smiled thinly. "I mean to ensure that they are all at dinner, from my son Paul to the chauffeur's family. We will all sit at the table together, family and staff. Even Bruno must come. We will make it an occasion. Before the end of the main course, you will excuse yourself and leave the dining room. The U.S. mail leaves Fifeness at eight-fifteen. By then you will be in Fifeness and the manuscript will be in the mail on its way to the airport and its publishers in New York, before anyone outside this room knows that it is completed. At eight-fifteen I will reach the climax of my little speech. If someone remembers earlier that you are missing, I will make sure that you are not followed."

"I will return quickly," Sergeant Freich promised, frowning. He went back to his duties, and I began to put my typewriter to bed for what I knew now was the last time.

"When will you leave here, Fräulein?" Johann Richter had taken out his checkbook and was writing at his desk.

"I thought in the morning, Herr Richter."

"I will be sorry to see you go. I have added a bonus to the amount we agreed upon, for you have more than carried out your part of the bargain. Will you return to California from this cold place? Or do you have something else in mind, perhaps to marry our young friend?"

"I have promised to marry him."

He smiled. "Then something good has come of this for you both. I am glad, Fräulein. Weather permitting, Connell will drive you to Fifeness in the morning. I hope you find happiness waiting there."

I thanked him and looked around the study where I had worked for months. There were unanswered questions here, but I did not care about that. It was over. They were no concern of mine now. Nobody had been hurt, and Rick waited in the village, where we had our own plans to make. My check was going to help. Johann had added a thousand dollars to the amount we had agreed upon, and although we had finished earlier than expected, he had paid the full amount originally quoted.

Back in my room I glanced at the clock. Ten minutes past four. Plenty of time before dinner to rest, bathe, and pack. I qualified that. To pack would be to alert Adrienne that the memoirs were finished. She wouldn't be able to tell Herman quickly enough. And he would tell Paul. I had left my check carelessly on the bedside table, too. Adrienne wasn't a girl to knock before she walked into my room. That was as telltale a signal as packing. I must be careful about things like this until Sergeant Freich left Valhalla tonight with the manuscript.

I hid my check safely away and lay down for an hour's rest. I wakened with Adrienne standing beside my bed, and was glad I'd put the check away.

"What's with the old man?" she demanded, looking at me with suspicion in her dark eyes. "Elsa said Sergeant Freich sent her back when she brought the afternoon coffee to the study. He said Herr Richter was resting and you were gone. Sergeant Freich told me the same thing when I went down to see if the old man needed me. Freich said he was just tired and resting. He didn't need the doctor, he didn't need me. Mostly he works till he's ready to drop. Now I find you here resting too. What's going on?"

"We're both tired," I said, smiling. "I'm too tired to crawl under the shower. Imagine how he must feel."

"The way you both work, you could finish sooner, couldn't you, Lorna?" she asked, watching me.

I yawned. "That's possible, I suppose." I tried not to make my voice wary, the way I felt.

"When do you expect to finish it? You can tell me," she urged.

"How long have I been here, Adrienne? I've lost count of time lately. I'm so tired I could have been here *years*."

"Slightly under four months," she said. "That's how long you've been here. And I asked you a question. When will you finish it?"

"My agreement says six months," I told her. "You say I've been here four. *You* work it out, Adrienne. I'm too tired to think. There's one thing, though. I never could do the impossible, like cramming six months' work into four. Could you?"

She sniffed and went back to her room, shutting the door behind her. Looking at the closed door, I decided it was going to be a lot easier to say good-bye to Adrienne this time than last. Because I couldn't sleep now, I switched on the transistor radio I'd brought from California. Among a lot of static I got the afternoon weather report. A blizzard was expected, sweeping down from the Newfoundland banks. It was already blanketing the west coast of Nova Scotia with snow and ice and was expected to hit the coast of Maine sometime this evening.

This evening? It was already here, blasting furiously at the walls and windows of Valhalla. It was as though my last night in the great stone house had suddenly become my first again. Shivering, I got up to put more wood on the open fire. The wind in the chimney showered me with sparks. Outside I could hear big seas already battering the rocks below the cliff road.

I went nervously into the bathroom to run my

hot bath. With the taps running, I went back to the bedroom and tried to phone Rick, reminding myself to be careful about what I said, as we had an electronics expert in the house—Paul. I needn't have bothered. The phone was out again, as dead as it had been that first night. Somewhere along the cliffs the line was already down. With Rick unavailable, I undressed and crawled into my bath, trying to find comfort there.

I heard Adrienne close her door while I was dressing. She went downstairs without even bothering to see if I was ready. Not that it mattered, I decided. Adrienne and I had lost what we had once shared—a close friendship. I took my time and walked slowly downstairs. The hot bath had revived me, but I was still aware of a dragging weariness.

"You look charming, Fräulein."

I turned in surprise, to see Johann Richter walking toward me from the direction of the kitchens. "Thank you, Herr Richter!"

Behind him I could hear excited female laughter coming from the kitchens, where plates clattered and appetizing smells crept into that end of the long passage.

"All goes well in the kitchen," he said cheerfully. "Erma is excelling herself, and Erma is a very good cook. There is a lot of curiosity. I hope you haven't satisfied any of it?"

"No, Herr Richter."

"Good!" he said. "Then we will walk in together. That way, it is I who will have to answer their questions. It may save you embarrassment."

He cocked his head to one side as I walked with my hand on the arm he had offered me with old-fashioned courtesy. He smiled and said, "Do you hear that? The house lives tonight!"

The living room was full of strange voices, I realized as we entered. Faces turned quickly to look at us. All the outside staff of Valhalla seemed to be there, sipping wine that a flushed and nervous Elsa and another maid were serving. I saw Herman coming toward us quickly, a half-empty whiskey glass in his hand, Adrienne following him through the crowd.

"Is this some crazy idea of yours, Father?" Herman demanded angrily. "Having the servants in here?"

"Mine, yes. Crazy, no, Herman," his father said calmly. "I feel like dining with my fellow country-men and -women tonight. There are some who are not German. Your friend, my little French nurse, Fräulein Courbet, Fräulein Mitchell, Connell over there. But in this house we all speak a common language—German. You don't know what day it is today, do you, Herman?"

"What day, Father?" Herman stared at him suspiciously.

"Today is an anniversary, Herman," he said sternly. "A year ago today we moved into this house that my agents had acquired for me."

"Is that all?" Herman asked deprecatingly.

"You do not think this important?" There were danger signals in Johann's voice.

"Of course, Father!" Herman retreated hastily. "I did not remember the date, that is all."

"Where is your brother?"

"He has been in his laboratory all day. He—"

"Bring him!" Johann snapped. "He should be here."

Herman left as though relieved to be gone. Johann was offering me champagne from a tray. I shook my head, but he gave it to me just the same. "You need only sip, Fräulein," he said. "It will relax you."

"*Prosit*, Herr Richter!" I hadn't noticed Sergeant Freich, but he was holding up a glass, Bruno standing firmly beside him. His eyes signaled, he nodded, and Johann smiled. Sipping, I decided the jeep must be ready. I didn't envy Sergeant Freich his drive to Fifeness tonight. But he would make it, I was sure. He was that kind of man.

Erma had come in, a tall and stately woman. She wore a long woolen frock, and there was no evidence that she had just been supervising a meal for twenty or more people in her kitchen.

"The dinner is ready when you are, Uncle Johann." She smiled.

He signaled the maid to bring her a glass of champagne. "We wait for Paul, Erma, then we go in. You have earned this. Do *you* know why we are having this little dinner tonight?"

She laughed. "I thought at first you had finished your book, Uncle Johann, but then I remembered we came to Valhalla about a year ago. I was not sure of the date, but I looked it up."

"You are smarter than Herman, Erma," he said

approvingly. "And here is Paul. We can go in to dinner now."

Paul walked to the bar and turned with a whiskey in his hand, frowning at the people filing past. Momentarily as I walked past him I had the impression that he wanted to stop me. He raised a hand, seemed about to say something, then let his hand fall. Relieved, I walked on with his father and Erma.

We sat at our usual places at the family table, with the other tables arranged so that Johann could see all of his entourage as they sat down. Connell, the chauffeur, was having trouble getting his three children seated. When he glanced apologetically at Johann and sat down himself, Johann rapped on the table for attention.

"Some of you may not remember that a year ago today we moved into this house," he said. "This is why I asked you here tonight. To refresh our memories and enjoy each other's company. Not as employers and employees, but as fellow Germans who have found a new life. Later in the dinner I will talk to you about this, and about certain plans I have for us all one day soon. In the meantime, enjoy yourselves, as I mean to do tonight." He raised his glass. "*Prosit!*"

"*Prosit!*"

"*Prosit,* Herr Richter!"

We had all raised our glasses, and the response and good wishes from the other tables appeared unanimous. But Johann said sternly, "Paul?"

Paul was frowning at his glass on the spotless tablecloth, the drink untouched. He looked at

Johann, stood up, and raised the glass. "To your health, Father," he said in an expressionless voice, and drained the glass.

Beside me Johann leaned back satisfied, and turned to say something to Erma on his other side. He never said it. The lights went out. One of the maids gasped at the sudden total darkness, and a glass shattered as it was dropped. For a long moment there was no sound in the room.

"The storm has given us a problem, it seems," Paul's raised voice said. "It will be better if everyone remains seated until it is adjusted. Connell, can you find your way through the kitchen and change over to the auxiliary power?"

"Yes, Herr Richter."

"There is a flashlight in the machine shed. You know where it is."

"This would happen tonight," Johann said beside me. "Well, we have a bad storm outside, and there is wine in the glasses if you can reach them without knocking things over. This should not take Connell long."

Someone laughed, and conversation started again. I noticed the faint glow of light showing through the ice on the windows. "The lights are still on in the hothouses, Herr Richter," I said.

"Paul installed his own power system there," he said, glancing at the window. "It was necessary because of the value of the plants and their rarity. You have seen them?"

"Yes. They're magnificent."

"Paul is responsible for the complete success of the conservatory and one of the finest collections of tropical plants in the world. Paul's heating system pumps hot air continuously into the greenhouses. Neither that nor the lighting system in there has ever failed. The whole system is entirely separate from the house. It cost a fortune, but it was worth it." He raised his voice. "Paul, Connell seems to be taking a long while."

"Too long," Paul's voice said from the complete darkness. "I hope the fault isn't in the house wiring. I heard the motor start, but nothing happened."

"Connell is coming now, Herr Richter!" one of the maids called from near the door.

Light flickered in the passage. It showed the diners seated at the tables briefly, before Connell shone his flashlight on the ceiling. "The auxiliary motor started, Herr Richter," he reported, "and the generator. I have a light in the machine shed, but nothing else. Power's off in the kitchen. No lights in the house. It has to be a fault in the house wiring somewhere."

"My dinner will spoil!" Erma muttered in dismay.

"How long would such a fault take to find and correct, Paul?" Johann asked anxiously.

"Who can say? Hours perhaps," Paul replied indifferently. "Your night is spoiled, Father." He hesitated. "Unless . . ."

"Unless what?" Johann asked angrily.

"We could dine in the conservatory in warmth and comfort. You've often had meals there while you catalog your flowers. Everything we need is there. There's a covered walk to the hothouses.

Work tables that we can convert quickly to dinner tables. Heat to keep Erma's dinner hot is there in plenty. And we have enough willing hands in this room to make the change before Erma's dinner can spoil."

"Brilliant!" Johann said in a pleased voice. "In the conservatory? Why not? Sometimes I think you are a genius, Paul."

"Others have been sure of that, Father," Paul's cold voice said. "Connell and I will run an extension from the laboratory into the passage, and another into the kitchen." He raised his voice. "Gerhardt and Schultz! You will clear the center hothouse except for the side benches, and all we will need is chairs. We'll have one long table and flowers all around it. Connell and I will organize heat for the dinner in the first hothouse. Erma, have the rest carry the food and wine in and set the table. Come with me, Connell, and give one of the maids your flashlight."

"My son is a born organizer," his father said admiringly. "This will be a dinner none of us will forget!"

In the kitchen there was light almost at once as Connell brought in a globe on a long extension lead. Another gave us sufficient light in the passage and dining room to see what we were doing. I found myself loaded with heavy silver cutlery from the table. Even Johann was carrying bottles of wine. We moved toward the passage, with Sergeant Freich close as always to Johann.

Momentarily we three were apart, and Sergeant

Freich said in a low voice, "I could go now, Herr Richter. In the confusion, none would miss me."

It seemed a good idea to me, as I remembered things I had forgotten. But Johann thought differently. "Wait," he said. "There is plenty of time, fortunately, so we will do this thing as we planned. That way, I will have everyone where I can see them when you leave."

"Ja, Herr Richter," Sergeant Freich muttered, falling back to a more respectful distance.

It was a brilliant idea of Paul's, I decided. The changeover went smoothly, with everyone suddenly enthusiastic and laughing like teenagers at a party after the first drink. The crowd had changed suddenly from the employer's family and the employees to just people at a party, truly enjoying themselves.

It was astonishing how quickly the move was completed. The benches on which the flowers had stood became tables covered with spotless tablecloths, shining wineglasses, and glittering silver. The chairs were a little crowded between the tables and the benches of flowers along the walls, but there was just room for the maids serving the first course of the dinner to move between.

"And now," Johann declared in his deep voice, "if you will all be seated, I think we should drink to my son Paul, don't you? Without his quick thinking, we might have had a dismal evening. Tell me, have you ever seen a more stunning setting for a dinner party?"

I looked around appreciatively. Our dining room was a place of breathtaking beauty. Insulated against the sound and fury of the storm, calm, warm, more lovely than any dining room any of us had ever seen. It was difficult to realize that outside the metal sheath protecting glass that sparkled in the light, a gale—indeed, now, as I heard Connell remark, a *blizzard*—was raging. Outside, the temperature was subzero; in here, tropical. It was like being in some fairy-tale palace with the diners surrounded by banks of beautiful and exotic flowers. The glass walls, sheathed, gleamed like diamonds in the bright light.

The maids giggled, squeezing behind us expertly to place plates of steaming soup or pour the wine that went with it.

"Now," Johann said with satisfaction, "is the time to drink to Paul, who made this possible." He had begun to stand up, glass in hand, when I saw one of the kitchen women hurry up and whisper to Erma.

"Uncle Johann," Erma cried in dismay. "Zelda says there is no heat for the main course, the St. Martin's goose!"

"Impossible," Johann said indignantly. "The heat never fails in here. Do you notice any change? Are you growing cold, Erma? What nonsense! I am hot!"

Paul frowned and stood up.

"Zelda could be right, Father," Paul said. "The heater they are using is a separate unit, not part of the heating system. It may have blown a fuse. If you will be patient for a moment, I'll get one from the lab and put it in. I know exactly where to look."

Paul began squeezing quickly past the other diners, without waiting for Johann to reply.

"It has never happened before, to my knowledge," Johann grumbled to his guests. "But there must always be a first time, eh? It is this verdammt blizzard! Elsa, bring more wine for everyone while we wait for Paul. At least we can be merry while we wait."

He sat down and turned to watch Paul, as others were doing. In the first greenhouse Paul had reached the excited kitchen women, all trying at once to tell him what had happened. He straightened and looked back at us and nodded as though to say: "Just as I thought. It is the fuse."

I watched him walk down the passage, open the laboratory door, and go inside. The door closed behind him.

Around the long table, voices were starting to rise excitedly. The wine had mellowed Adrienne. She was smiling as she sipped. She noticed me looking at her and giggled. "Isn't it fantastic?"

It was the wine, of course. Even Sergeant Freich's brown face was redder than usual, though he hadn't been drinking like the others. In the sergeant's case, I decided, it was probably the unaccustomed warmth in the conservatory. Paul had told me the greenhouses were kept at a temperature in excess of eighty degrees Fahrenheit. We who lived in the big stone house were not used to that. All winter the huge, bleak rooms had been almost twenty degrees colder. Over there we needed our log fires.

I realized unexpectedly, though, that it seemed

to be growing cooler in the greenhouse. The warm inflow of air was colder, and there was something about it . . . I sniffed curiously, and discovered that it seemed to have acquired a faintly chemical smell, barely perceptible among the perfumes of our exotic flowers. But that could be my imagination. Down at the end of the table the wife of one of the gardeners was about to fall asleep. Her head started to nod, and as I watched, she drooped forward with her head on the table. I decided that was Johann's fault as I saw her husband notice and begin to shake her angrily. Johann was giving them too much wine.

I turned to Johann, but he was staring straight ahead, frowning at Adrienne, who had her head on the table and had spilled her soup, for it was staining the tablecloth and the sleeve of her dress. Something was wrong in here, something . . . Suddenly terrified, I tried to get up, but there was no strength in my arms and legs. I stopped straining and lolled back in my chair like a rag doll. And as I looked at Johann Richter, he too started leaning backward wearily in his chair.

Next to where Adrienne sprawled on the table, Herman had disappeared. I saw his hand reach up slowly from where he had fallen and grip the edge of the table, trying to drag himself up. But as I watched, the clawing fingers relaxed, the hand fell back.

I noticed that even Bruno was lying languidly on the floor, his head drooped over his massive paws.

I screamed in panic, calling to the only one I thought might help us.

"Hans! Hans . . . Freich! Help us!"

He too looked as drowsy as the other men who were still upright. But he heard me. My head lolled back, and I seemed to lose the power of speech, for though I tried to call to him again, no sound came. But he had heard and understood. The muscles in his jaws corded. He was forcing himself slowly upright, out of the chair, erect. He began dragging himself along by the table edge toward where Johann and I sat at the head of the table. Diners fell away before his ponderous advance, toppling, falling, their chairs overturning.

He reached Herman and trampled ponderously over him as he had the others. Adrienne's chair fell to one side, and he was standing opposite where I sat, extending one hand as though to help Johann. He let his hand fall.

Braced there with his hands gripping the edge of the table, he looked at me and shook his head.

"I cannot . . . help you! Auschwitz! He told me once Paul was there!"

He was leaving me, forcing himself erect, moving as though in slow motion toward the first greenhouse. Toppling Erma Richter from his path, he struggled on. Bruno strained to get to his feet and follow his master. But the effort was too demanding, and he fell back on the floor, snarling, then was suddenly still.

Hans Friech's progress was marked by falling, breaking pots, spilling the glory of their flowers upon the floor as he hauled himself along by the benches. I saw him reach the first greenhouse. Slowing, but still moving, he got to the passage. He stopped, leaning against the laboratory door, groping beneath his coat.

Paul could see him on the closed-circuit television, I remembered. Paul must know everything he was doing. He wasn't going to be able to open Paul's door or the door leading into the house. They were of metal, locked, sealed against the escape of gas.

But that was a gun Hans Freich was taking from beneath his coat. He had to use both hands to raise it, to press it against the lock of the door. The gun boomed, the sound shattering in this sealed shell of metal in which I sat. It boomed again against the lock, and a third time. He dropped the gun then, and it fired from the jar of its fall upon the concrete floor, though where the bullet went, I had no idea. But he could not bend to pick up the fallen gun. He turned away in one last, desperate effort that carried him staggering to the passage door.

He began to beat on it with his great hands as though trying to hammer his way through it into the fresh air inside the house. But he had spent his strength. His blows weakened, died. For a moment longer he clung to the door, then slid down.

Beside me, as Hans Freich fell and lay still, I heard Johann Richter's breath sigh out despairingly, as though he too saw what happened and understood as I did. He too, I realized, could see and hear. But we could neither speak nor move. We were breathing shallowly, but how long could we do so? I began to hear sound somewhere; I was not sure where. The movement of my eyes, like the rest of my body, was becoming paralyzed now.

I saw then that the laboratory door had opened and closed, and a strange figure was bending over Hans Freich, taking things from his pocket. When it straightened, I saw that the figure wore a scuba diver's aqualung and mask. It turned to stare down the length of the three greenhouses at the kitchen women sprawled on the floor, at the long table where nothing moved. It came toward me, walking quickly.

Horrified, I watched him approach, to bend over me. A hand raised my head and looked at my face. Through the glass I recognized Paul Richter. His lips moved, but I could not hear what he was saying through the mask. He rested my head back against the chair and turned to his father. When he straightened, he held keys in his hand. The keys of his father's study and the wall safe. Walking quickly, he went back through the hothouses into the laboratory. The door closed.

It was becoming very cold. There was no longer air flowing past, though the faint smell of chemicals still lingered. I imagined Paul finding the manuscript in the safe or somewhere in Johann's rooms.

I listened for the sound of the jeep driving away, and faintly above the wind and sleet I heard it coming around the house to stop near the side door.

He would leave us now, I thought. Leave the gas to do its work. We would die, but they would find and punish him for what he had done to us. Poison gas left traces in the lungs and blood, easily detected.

I had almost slipped into unconsciousness when a sound awakened me. It had grown freezing cold. My eyes, focusing, saw the bare glass of the wall in front of me, the light through it showing me snow and icicles on the neighboring trees and the ground. The sound that had awakened me was the retracting of the metal sheet that protected the greenhouses, leaving the glass exposed.

I tried to cry out in terror, but no sound came as something driven on the wind struck the glass wall I was looking at and cracked it. And almost at once there was the sound of rending, shattering glass above. The branch of a tree fell across where Herman and Adrienne lay on the other side of the table. Glass showered down on us from the broken roof. I listened to another crash and another. Something soft and cold touched my face. White fluff wavered past my eyes, settling on the tablecloth, settling on the black hair of one of the gardeners' wives farther down the table.

Snow!

Horrified, I tried to scream, to force myself upright as Hans Freich had done and escape from this horrible complex of greenhouses where we had been paralyzed and now were being killed by cold and exposure. It was as though I was living my first night here all over again. Paul Richter was killing me now as he had intended to kill me then. The cold was becoming more intense every moment.

Other debris kept crashing through the remnants of roof. Ice cascaded inside; ice gathered on the protective metal shield, now falling through the broken roof and walls. It began to build up with sleet carried on the wind. I felt drowsier and drowsier. The gardener's wife's hair had turned white. A sliver of falling glass had cut Johann's hand, but he was no longer bleeding. I had heard that the dead do not bleed. . . .

Somewhere I imagined I heard a man's laughter. A motor revved and drove away.

It occurred to me that Paul did not have to run from his crime. He could say truthfully we had dined in the hothouses. That was obvious. He would say there had been a power failure. He could prove that. He often fed gas into the hot-air system to destroy fungi and bacteria on the plants. He used gas as a pesticide. He would say, and prove, that the electronic control had malfunctioned and fed the gas into the system while we sat at dinner. The same electronic malfunction, worsening, had caused the protective sheathing to retract, exposing the glass.

The storm had done the rest.

He was on his way to Fifeness. And we were not yet dead. Who could say at what hour we died? He would be seen in the village. He could come back in the morning. He could bring witnesses, and they would think it was just as he said. He would be as shocked as they at such a tragedy.

It did not matter what he said, I decided. That couldn't help us.

We were dead.

★ *Epilogue* ★

I awakened in my bedroom in Valhalla. A log
fire blazed on the hearth, and someone sitting on
the edge of my bed was massaging my frozen
hands and arms and muttering endearing things
in a familiar voice. It took effort to open my heavy
eyes and look at Rick, his expression so anxious
that I wanted to cry. But he saw me and was lift-
ing me into his arms, hugging me.

"Thank God!" he muttered, and just kept right
on hugging me and saying that over and over until someone tapped on my door and came in. Over
Rick's shoulder I recognized Sheriff Walton's grim
face.

"How is she, Rick?"

"She just opened her eyes," Rick said. "Dr.
Brewster saw her. He said she's suffering from exposure and shock mainly. He thinks the effect of
whatever gas Richter used is wearing off now. No
broken bones or other injuries."

"She's luckier than some of the others. Can she
speak yet? Some can, some can't."

All Rick's anxiety came back as he looked at
me.

185

"I can . . . speak!" I whispered, but it took effort, and what I said didn't sound right to me.

"Good!" Sheriff Walton reached out a big hand to pat my shoulder. "You're safe, Miss Mitchell, and you're going to be all right."

But there was something I had to tell him. "Paul . . . Richter! Don't let him . . . get away!" It took so much of my strength saying it that I began to fade away again.

"He didn't get away," Sheriff Walton said. "He can't harm or frighten you again, Miss Mitchell." He lowered his voice. "Rick, we're about ready to move out. I've plenty of help now. We'll move out in convoy along the cliff road. The ambulances will go straight through to the county hospital. You want me to send up a stretcher?"

"I'll carry her down," Rick said. "She's coming home with me."

Valhalla was full of deputies as Rick carried me downstairs to the waiting car. The living room looked like an emergency hospital, with people wrapped in blankets lying everywhere, doctors and nurses working over them. The lights were on, the sabotaged wiring repaired. Rick would not allow me to talk in the sheriff's car. Not that I wanted to, because I was warm and comfortable in Rick's arms. And when I reached the widow's house, Dr. Brewster was there. He gave me a shot that put me to sleep. It wasn't till the next day that I learned how we were miraculously saved from that horrible ice palace of dead flowers and frozen food.

Rick was responsible for our escape and the prevention of planned mass murder by an expert. Rick had met the chauffeur's wife in the village and learned Paul hadn't gone to the Connell house on my first night in Fifeness when I almost died on the cliff road. Suspicion growing, Rick went to the gas station. He learned from the mechanic there that Paul had taken home the battery which he had told me Connell was supposed to pick up. The mechanic volunteered to put it in, but Paul refused his offer. Paul said he would put it in himself when the old battery ran out.

Rick told the sheriff this, but Walton thought it insufficient evidence. Determined to take me away from there, Rick tried to call me at Valhalla, but the phone was dead. Frantic for my safety, he kept pestering the sheriff until Walton finally agreed to drive Rick out to talk to the chauffeur and his wife. The two cars started out together, Sheriff Walton on his way to Valhalla to interrogate the Connells, and Paul Richter on his way to Fifeness to establish his alibi.

The sheriff's car was turning into the Devil's Bend when it met Paul Richter driving at high speed toward Fifeness. To avert an accident the sheriff switched on his rooftop flashing light, stopped the car, and tried to flag Paul down.

Recognizing the flashing light, Paul thought at once that someone had survived the mass murder he intended and had contacted police. In the split-second decision his guilt forced him to make, Paul swung the wheel of the jeep and went down into the sea. Even as I learned these things from Rick, police were recovering Paul's body. Searching, they found a few leaves of the manuscript, but except for a few odd words the sea had washed the record of the life and times of Johann Richter from its pages.

There were three other fatalities on that dreadful night. Johann Richter was dead, the cold too much for his weakened body. And Hans Freich and Bruno, who had given so much loyalty, were dead with him. The mighty effort he made to get into the laboratory had been too much even for the great heart of Sergeant Hans Freich.

I was asked many questions about the manuscript, which I answered truthfully. It ended there. My questioners went away. Herman Richter, suddenly a very, very wealthy man, left with Adrienne for Europe the day the inquest was over. They married there. I sometimes wonder if Adrienne is happy. I know I am. I have discovered that I have a very talented husband.

Only, sometimes in dreams I hear Hans Freich saying: "I cannot help you! Auschwitz! He told me once Paul was there!"

And I remember the last time Paul was mentioned in the memoirs. Paul had been sent to Oswiecim from his chemical-research command in Zabrze, Poland.

I know now that Oswiecim is Auschwitz, and that multitudes of innocent people died there from piped-in deadly gas.